MW01601853

X Dames

A Lucy Ripken Mystery

ALSO BY J. J. HENDERSON

Murder on Naked Beach

Mexican Booty

X Dames

A Lucy Ripken Mystery

J. J. Henderson

cds
BOOKS

New York

Published by CDS Books

Text design by Ruth Lee-Mui

Library of Congress Cataloging-in-Publication Data

Henderson, J. J.
    X Dames : a Lucy Ripken mystery / J. J. Henderson.
        p.   cm.
    ISBN-13: 978-1-59315-289-5 (pbk. : alk. paper)
    ISBN-10: 1-59315-289-2 (pbk. : alk. paper) 1. Women
photographers—Fiction. 2. Reality television programs—Fiction.
3. Mexico—Fiction. I. Title.
PS3608.E526X3 2006
813'.6—dc22   2006019421

CDS books are available at special discounts for bulk purchases in the U.S. by corporations, institutions, and other organizations. For more information, please contact the Special Markets Department at the Perseus Books Group, 11 Cambridge Center, Cambridge, MA 02142, or call (800) 255-1514 or (617) 252-5298, or email special.markets@perseusbooks.com.

06 07 08 09 / 10 9 8 7 6 5 4 3 2 1

For DD and Jade

Acknowledgments

Thanks to my friend Geoff Harris for insights into the world of reality television.

X Dames

A Lucy Ripken Mystery

1

Escape from New York

Lucy happened to be standing in the kitchen staring at the main event, a semi-defrosted package of sliced turkey breast, when Harry called at nearly five p.m.—unforgivably late as usual—to make excuses for not making it to dinner that night, voice crackling through a cell phone from somewhere in the vicinity of Caracas, Venezuela. Or so he claimed. Before she could hang up on him, he got his story going and she had to admit it was a good one. It seems, he told her, that these two dope guys he knew from his bad old days in Provincetown once upon a time had buried a million in cocaine-generated cash in heavy-duty plastic bags exactly 120 meters due north of the northeast corner of a gas station on the edge of a small town called Snake Creek, near the northern edge of Everglades National Park. So they'd told him, years back.

The first guy had his head blown off in a dope-related shoot-out on a Bahama islet on New Year's Eve in 1999, and now Harry's sources had the second guy dead, heart stopped by a self-injected speedball sitting with the shades drawn, midday in a West Hollywood apartment. A miserable fate for a guy pushing sixty, Harry noted; but in any case, he went on, they'd told him about the stash of cash at least ten years ago, when he was in transition from bad boy to good cop, and at the time they'd both insisted, should they bite the dust, that no else knew and he should help himself to the money when the statute of limitations ran out. Now they were dead and it had. Harry didn't see a whole lot of excess moral weight attached to the bags of cash, and so—"Harry, that's enough," Lucy said. "Just cut me ten percent for stress and suffering when you dig it up."

"No problem, Luce," he said. "I could even go twelve. But there's more. Because once I was there, in Florida I mean, guess what? Or should I say guess who," he added, intriguingly, "got me from Florida to Venezuela?" He paused. "Do the initials 'MV' ring any chimes?"

"MV?" Lucy pondered. A truck squalled downstairs, gridlocked. "God, I've got to get out of here," she said. "I'm going utterly insane." A light dawned. "Maria Verde? You're after Maria Verde?"

"Was," Harry said, disappointment surfacing. "There was a reported sighting. I was in Florida to organize my dig—unfortunately the gas station is gone, in fact the tire department of a Wal-Mart appears to be positioned precisely atop the spot where the cash is supposedly buried, so I think it might stay buried for a while yet—when my *amigo Rogelio el Camarón*—"

"Roger the Shrimp?" Lucy asked. "This is a guy you never mentioned before."

"He is possessed, they say, of the largest tool in Latin America."

"And proud of it no doubt."

"He used to be a cop. Now he's a porn star, hefting the heaviest wood south of the Rio Grande. But he's always done right by me, from way back when. And naturally I had red flagged that psycho-bitch, right after Jamaica. So Roger called to inform me that a person looking very much like our Maria recently had been seen on a plane headed out of Rio bound for Caracas. There was even video footage from an airport security camera. I saw it, and I do believe it was possibly her, although the shades and hair were very large. So I zipped down, only to find the trail gone cold. But here I am."

"Yes, there you are," said Lucy. "And here I am, not liking the thought of Maria Verde one bit, and wondering who's going to help me eat the three pounds of turkey fajitas I planned on cooking."

"Your friend Mickey seems to have a reliable appetite," Harry said.

"That's true—or was true, anyways, until she recently started taking antidepressants and went on a crash-and-burn diet."

"Mickey on a diet! You're kidding!"

"Her butt had gotten epic, Harry. And now the girl has lost twenty-seven pounds. Some kind of South Beach meets Atkins meets Weight Watchers in hell. She's on drugs, plus she met a guy and got inspired. No booze, no carbs, no fat, no fun—God, the forbidden list is endless. She's not good company right now, to tell the truth. I think when she hits 140 or so she'll start eating again. Or if he dumps her like the usual suspects usually do. Meanwhile—"

"Hey, sorry, Luce. Really. Trust me. I am not in Venezuela because I want to be."

"Sure, Harry. I'll share dinner with the dog." She sighed. "At least he's reliable."

"What can I say, it's—"

"I know, I know, not your fault. Listen, call me when you get back. I gotta go."

"Later Luce." He hung up. She clicked off and almost threw the phone. Damn that guy. Why did she still see him, when she never knew when she'd see him again?

The word for this moment was—*whatever*. She poked the turkey breast. It hadn't really defrosted. She shoved it back in the freezer, bagged all the neatly sliced and diced vegetables and put them in the refrigerator, stuck her cell phone in her purse, then took off her sexy black translucent lounging jammies and put on a pair of modified homeboy street pants, cut to ride high because Lucy was decidedly not into butt cleavage or pubic hairstyling. She added a neo-hippie beaded top, a little black sweater, her black cat's-eye glasses, and open-toed sandals, for the late April breeze wafting in the windows carried early hints of summer. She woke the sleeping poodle with a "Yo, Claud, wanna hit it?" He leaped up and scrambled for the door. She checked makeup, brushed her currently medium-long blonde hair back, did lipstick, grabbed leash and purse and headed out, not forgetting to lock the door.

She tripped five flights down—the elevator had been out of commission for a month—and out the building door onto her beloved, kinetic, once-funky Broadway— transformed, before her very eyes, from downscale shopping paradise to street-front shopping mall. Pseudo-hip corporate retail stores lined the street on both sides, in both directions, as far as her eye could see. Chasing after trendiness by moving into SoHo, these enterprises ended up chasing the trendies right out of the neighborhood. But that had been going on downtown long before Lucy Ripken had moved in, and she knew it was the inevitable evolution of the city. If bands of murderous, airplane-hijacking suicidal terrorists couldn't change the economic dynamic, no one could. And they had failed, thank God. But still, the damned street used to have some soul, or at least some cheap places to buy clothing and food, and now it was ruled by corporate retail.

She leashed the big white poodle, quite dashing with his newly shorn spring hair and his brilliant brown eyes, and walked west on Broome, then north on Wooster and west on Spring, dodging the packs of irksome wannabe hipsters and overdressed Eurotrash shoppers and noisy New Jersey noshers and the occasional haunted-looking longtime SoHo resident, belatedly maneuvering baby- and grocery-packed stroller home through the once serene, dignified blocks. Lucy was headed for the sylvan banks of the Hudson, and on the way she emptied herself of all the things that currently worried her: Harry, the demise of her neighborhood, the flatlining sales of her Mexican book, the state of the union and the world. A girl could go nuts pondering the last, she thought, then let it go as a warm breeze rippled over from the river. On the other hand, she couldn't quite let go of the image of Maria Verde, with her cockeyed Kewpie-doll grin, snarling in Jamaican moonlight as she pointed a gun at Lucy's heart. Lucy had been maybe ten seconds from dead when Harry's "associate" Prudence Fallowsmith, Jamaican cop, had tackled the raving, gun-toting bitch, saving Lucy's life. Maria Verde, whose drug deal Lucy and Harry had foiled, disappeared up the beach, and that was the last Lucy had seen or heard of her until today. They had stopped the drug deal, but still, Maria Verde had gotten away with murder.

In the soft spring evening, with traffic hushed to a white roar, and the crowds of SoHo now behind her, Lucy let Maria Verde go as well.

Soon she crossed the Westside Highway and turned south on the ped and bike path. Forty minutes from her noisy front door, she settled on a bench under the lush green trees of Battery Park. She gazed out, watching boats slide up and down the river as the lights of Jersey City rose before her.

As she considered what to do about dinner, and Claud lazily chased the odd squirrel, and children played amidst the quirky bestiary of miniature statues in the park, she loved New York again for a minute. Then her cell phone rang, an organ riff snatched from an ancient Los Lobos song, "Kiko and the Lavender Moon." She quickly fished it out of her purse and flipped it open. "Lucy here."

"That would be Lucy Ripken?"

"Yeah. Who's calling?" A female, didn't sound like a telemarketer, but you never knew.

"Hey chill out. It's me. Terry. Teresa MacDonald, you paranoid dame."

"Terry! Hey!" Terry lived in LA, wrote art criticism, had dated eccentric art-world celebs for years, and ranked among the smartest people Lucy knew. A still-skinny reformed anorexic, red-haired, athletic, neurotic as hell but loads of fun. They'd met when Lucy did a piece for an LA magazine called *SCRUB*, devoted to bathing arcana, that had a moment of trendy glory and then went down the drain when the publisher made the mistake of moving the operation to New York, where the sharks made short work of it. Terry had been the culture editor in *SCRUB*'s glory years. Year. *SCRUB* was a short-lived phenom. Lucy had the complete set of back issues in a small box stuck in the depths of her closet. But she and Terry had stayed friendly. "What's up, girl?"

"Not too much. Still working on Milton Schamberg."

"God, how's that going?" A few years ago, Terry had started on an exhaustive biography of an obscure mid-twentieth-century Southern California painter whom she decided had played a far larger role in the cultural evolution of Los Angeles than anyone knew. It was taking forever.

"I'm into his thirties, so . . . "

"Since he died at forty-four you must be close."

"But the good parts are still to come."

"Right. The sixties and all that. Have you managed to get anyone to underwrite you yet?"

"Grants are fewer and farther between than ever, especially in publishing, so the short answer is no. But—and this is why I'm calling you, Lucy—I've been scrambling for money as usual, and thanks to Milton's son—"

"His son?"

"He's a Hollywood guy. In his forties—or fifties. Who can tell around here? Anyway he's a sick fuck but connected. So anyways I've got an interesting offer, and as soon as I heard it I thought of you."

"Really? What's the deal?"

"What do you think of when I say X Dames?"

"X Dames? Um—pompous porn stars?"

"No, you goon. Don't you know about the X Games?"

"Sure. That's like radical skateboarding, right?"

"And snowboarding, surfing, mountain biking, kite sailing—all those crazy sports that started in Southern California and are now taking over the world. At least those parts wired for cable."

"So—"

"Mix that with buff babes in bikinis and voilà: a new reality TV show coming soon to your local cable channel, to be called the *X Dames*. A bunch of cute athletic women—a shifting cast of characters, depending on the sport and the locations and the available breast-enhanced-yet-athletic broads, I suspect—travel around to different places and engage in competitions. Surfing, biking, whatever. Between contests they're theoretically up to the usual backbiting, catfighting, bitch-slapping, and the other thrills and chills that make reality TV so enticing. To win *dólares*, trips to exotic foreign lands, dates with C-list TV actors. It's basic trash, but there's cash behind this trash. It seems kinda fun, and I have been anointed an associate producer-slash-writer with hiring power. So—you want a job?"

"You want to hire me? To do what?" Lucy stood and walked over to the railing to look down into the dark waters of the river. This was getting interesting.

"Reality TV is not always reality, Luce. I'm sure you know that. And this particular show is going to be fairly heavily scripted. But for some obscure reason they want to use only writers who've never worked in the Industry—hence the hire of yours truly, since I have never been near the TV biz, as you know—and the green light for me to hire you."

"So where does Milton Junior fit in?"

"He's the man behind the brilliant idea. He lives on top of Tuna Canyon, in his dad's old house."

"Right, the one that looks like a flying saucer. Isn't that where—"

"His mother fell to her death."

"Or was pushed."

"That's in my next chapter. But junior—his name is Bobby Schamberg, by the way, not Milton—doesn't seem to have a problem living with mommy's ghost. Especially since the pad has five bedrooms and a pool and views of the ocean you wouldn't believe. The original American Schambergs made it big in lighting fixtures in Chicago a hundred years ago, and Milton surprised us all—well, me, anyway, since I always assume little-known artists must be starving—by being, behind his Bohemian façade, a stock market whiz. He left a pile of dough that Bobby's been spending as fast as he can trying to play Hollywood. He's got a production company and thus far he's done a pair of seriously bad cable TV movies and a few sitcom pilots. The *X Dames* is his latest gambit. His ex-wife and current partner used to be a surfing champion, and they came up with the concept together. Since I was a writer and they knew me—I've been nosing around their lives for several years now, researching the book, and I think Bobby actually trusts me—they approached me, and I kind of helped them organize the initial proposal. Maybe they knew I needed money and did it out of pity. I don't know. In any case, they found some backers, pitched the thing to the Outside Network, where Bobby had a friend, and the next thing you know they got green-lighted and I got a sort of—job." She stopped. Lucy waited. "So what do you think?"

"Does this mean I get to get out of New York for the summer?"

"Like next week. Now. And you can bring your dog. I've got you set up in a studio two blocks from the beach in Venice if you take the offer. It's tiny and two thousand a month but the producers are willing to pay you about five times that, at least while they get the thing off the ground. You've got a bit of a rep thanks to the Mexico book—speaking of which, we have to go to Mexico right away because they want to jump-start the show by staging a surfing contest in this little town north of Puerto Vallarta called

Sayulita, and they tell me it's a north and west swell beach, so the waves will stop breaking once summer settles in."

"Jesus," said Lucy, awash in immediate and very cool possibilities. LA, working in TV, good money, another trip to Mexico, but this time the west coast, keeping those Isla Mujeres ghosts at bay a thousand miles away. A job! "It sounds too good to be true. Wow, Terry, I can't believe you pulled this off."

"I can't either. It fell on my head like a gold brick."

"I should say let me think about it for a couple of days, but I'm more inclined, right now, to say, see you next week. I just have to deal with my loft and—"

"Perfect. I'll tell them to email you a draft contract. You can read it, make changes, print it out, sign it, and send it back to me. Trust me, it'll treat you right."

"*Bueno*. And Terry, thanks for thinking of me."

"I've seen you on a sailboard, Luce. You could probably be an X Dame yourself, were you so inclined."

"No way, Ter. I'm pushing thirty-five and way too Manhattanized for competition sports."

"But still, you know your way around the ocean."

"I guess. Listen, I gotta go get a bite. My dinner guest— none other than the fabulous Harry Ipswich—putzed out on me, so I'm wandering the streets in search of food."

"Again!? Doesn't he do that all the time?"

"His schedule is—unpredictable. And so I suffer. Instead of cooking for him I'm going to my favorite bistro and see what looks good. Wish you could join me."

"Cook up an X Dame location in New York and I will. Meanwhile next week we'll make the LA dining rounds. I still hate TV, but it is nice to be getting a lot of money for a little work."

"Instead of a little money for a lot of work, the writer's usual fate. See you then." Lucy shut her phone, jumped in the air, and laughed out loud. "Claud, we are moving to Southern California!"

Fifteen minutes later, as she tethered Claud to a streetlamp and strolled into The Frog's Grotto, her Tribeca bistro of the moment, it dawned on her that at ten grand a month she'd make her twelve percent of Harry's buried million in a year. She had no illusions that the gig would last that long, but even a couple of months at ten thousand per would add up to a pile of money. And getting out of Manhattan for the summer was, quite simply, priceless.

When Harry showed up three days later, tanned, tired, dirty, and bug-bitten, Lucy couldn't help but feel a low glimmer of satisfaction when she told him she was moving to LA for a while. "And of course you're welcome to the loft, as always," she added, handing him an ice-crusted shot glass of his favorite vodka. Harry had a mouse-sized fourth-floor East Village walk-up, a *très chic* locale but short on amenities, with a tub in the kitchen and a toilet down the hall. Staying at Lucy's loft, with or without her there, was like a vacation for him. "And you don't even have to deal with the dogster. He's going with me, eh what, Claud? He'll be thrilled to see you when you come visit."

"Not so fast, kiddo," Harry said, and knocked back the shot. "Whooo, that's good." She poured him another. "Aside from the fact that I think you're crazy to go out there—LA is an inferno, Luce, and the TV industry inhabits the ninth circle—I've got my own out-of-town gig going. As it turns out, I'm on assignment in Florida for a while."

"What? What kind of assignment? You said you were done with Florida for now."

"Well, actually I volunteered for surveillance duty on a couple of illicit landing strips in the jungle not far from Snake Creek. My cover is I'm doing a piece on Everglades National Park for an airline magazine. But there is a ton of dope coming into the area by plane all the time, so I'll have my hands full. Who knows, I might even stop a few hundred pounds of coke or junk from finding its nasty way up here. But aside from that and the writing gig, the real reason I set it up is I've come up with a plan. I've been contemplating that Wal-Mart situation I told you about, with the million bucks, and I think I know a way to get at the money without—"

"You can't be serious, Harry. I've never been in a Wal-Mart, but I imagine there's probably fifty tons of concrete sitting on top of your mythical bags of money, plus security up the wazoo."

"Exactly. Security. As in seriously underpaid dudes in blue shirts with tin badges who would probably be very happy to get ten percent of my gross in exchange for getting me floor and fixture plans, and maybe running some cover, so that when I dig my tunnel from the swamp behind the back of the building I won't hit any cables, pipes, or people. I checked it out. There's a thick stand of jungle back there and the tunnel will only have to be about sixty or seventy feet long."

"A seventy-foot tunnel under a Wal-Mart superstore? Harry, you're nuts. This sounds like a really dumb-ass plan."

"You know what, Luce? Believe it or not, I'm sick of being broke all the time. Sick of living in that overpriced rat hole on East Seventh. I need a leg up and those guys weren't bullshitting me. The money's there for the taking, it's not stealing, and I'm the only person on the planet who knows about it. Excepting you, of course."

"It's a hare-brained scheme, Harry, and you know it. Besides, what am I going to do about the loft? Who can I get to stay here? I depend on you for this. You know I can't just advertise for a subletter. Not with the landlord situation."

"Hey, you're going to be working in TV. Making major money, right? If I were you, I'd just leave it empty. You can afford six hundred a month for the peace of mind."

She hadn't thought of that. Maybe it was true. She just wasn't used to that kind of spare cash. "Well, I'm going to make a few calls, see if I can round up someone trustworthy. If not, I guess I could just lock the door and walk away."

"Ask Jane downstairs to keep an eye on the place. She's kind of a friend, right? But I would take all your valuables and personal stuff. You never know what that fucking landlord might try."

Soon they cut the chatter and commenced with peeling each other's clothing off, a ritual that had only improved with time. By now, two years into it, they knew each other's hot spots, when and how to hit them. They spent that night together, and had great sex. Twice, with a vodka break between. Not at all bad for a fortysomething man and a thirtysomething girl. Even if she did kind of watch the clock, wondering. If her time was running out. Time for what? Love and marriage and a baby carriage? Who knew anymore these days?

Whatever Harry had in the way of failings, he was a wonderful lover and had been since their very first nights together in Jamaica. Lucy suspected his unpredictable availability had something to do with it—that hoary old cliché, absence makes the heart grow fonder, having some bearing on the situation. He was definitely absent.

Come morning, Harry went off to his East Village dump to prep for his own incipient departure back to the Florida swamps. Lucy got on the phone to chase after subletters while breaking out her three suitcases and two duffel bags, having decided to do a major reassessment of her worldly goods, so that what she took to California would be all that she held dear, and what she left behind would be the basics.

Everything else she bagged for throwaway, including the collected back issues of *SCRUB* magazine. By the time she was ready to go a week later, she had sixteen bags of trash, five overstuffed suitcases, and a loft that had never looked better—empty of everything but furniture, a couple of prints, her five-year-old dinosaur desktop PC—drained of all her files—and the essentials in the kitchen and bathroom.

She never did find anyone she trusted enough to sublet or loft-sit. In the first week of May—with a signed hard copy of her $2,500-per-week *X Dames* contract in her carry-on and a backup in her laptop—on the day before her departure to LA, she ambled downstairs and after walking Claud around the block, she went into the building next door. She tied Claud up and ascended to the second floor, where the bad-cop landlord Itzak Lascovich ran his business, SeaBee Fabric Merchants, out of a grubby little office in the corner of a dingy, fluorescent-lit, six-thousand-square-foot loft crammed with chaotically heaped twelve-foot rolls of cheap fabric. He dealt primarily with wholesalers in Africa, he claimed, but it was strange—in all her years in the loft she had never actually seen any fabric go into, or out of, his place of business. Only him, scurrying about in his rodent-like fashion.

She picked her way through the stacks of rolled fabric until she could see him through the dirty glass door of his office. He was greenish under the twittering lights, barking at someone on the phone, pushing his greasy white hair back with a clawlike hand. She tapped on the glass. He looked up, waved her in, continued barking. She opened the door. His wife—twice his size, thin brown hair pulled back tight, gaudy lipstick in place, tree-trunk legs nicely stockinged and crossed—never said a word and sat there vigilant as she did all day every day. She glared at Lucy briefly, then returned her gaze to the middle distance. Lascovich waved at the one chair not covered by papers, fabric samples, his skinny ass, or his wife's fat one. Lucy sat, feeling rather sassy in spite of the grim vibe in the grim little room. How they could spend fifty or sixty hours a week in this hole she had never figured out. "Goodbye," he said to the phone, then hung up. "So Miss Lucy Ripken it is the third of May you haf my rent?"

"I do, yes." She put the check on his desk. He picked it up, looked at it, frowned, and shook his head. "Sometime you will pay market value, Miss Lucy Ripken."

"Not this year." She smiled at him. "Don't forget it was you that initiated the lawsuit, Izzy."

"You are illegal. The whole lot of you. And I will get my buildink back sometime."

"Well, maybe so, but not today. Oh, by the way," she went on, hoping her casual tone would carry the moment. She had decided that though it would be risky to reveal her plans, it would be better than having Jane spring it on him after she was gone. This way, at least, she would have some idea of his response—and she could then deal accordingly. "I wanted to let you know that I'm going to be traveling for a while, and the place won't be occupied. But I will be paying rent, through Jane Aronstein, so you don't need to—"

"You can't go away and keep my floor for you to come back and—"

"Of course I can, Itzak. I will be paying the rent and—"

"If the place is not occupied then I am having it."

"I don't think so, Mr.—"

"I don't care what you are thinking, I am—"

"This conversation is over, Iz. I'll have my lawyer call you."

"No. I will be taking the place when you—"

"Good day, Mrs. Lascovich," she said, and breezed out. Then stormed down the stairs. "Damn," she said to Claud as she unhooked his leash from the banister, slammed out the door, and stood on the Broadway sidewalk, trying to collect herself. "Goddamn, pup," she said. "That guy is so infuriating."

She went into her own building, hiked up to her loft, and got on the phone with Jack Harshman, who'd been her legal pit bull on matters residential since the day she moved into the loft and Lascovich tried to evict her.

Later, after hours, she put all of her trash out on the street in black plastic bags, and then she did what Harshman had advised. She spent two hundred and fifty dollars to have a locksmith come over and hike up the stairs and change one of the three locks on her door and on the door inside the elevator at the other end of the loft. She gave a set of new keys to her downstairs neighbor Jane, with strict instructions not to let Lascovich or anyone else have them under any circumstances. Jane had been in the building even longer than Lucy so she got it. Lucy pocketed the other set.

After a less-than-rousing overnighter with Harry, whose excessive, mournful vodka drinking rendered him entirely incapable, they left for LaGuardia at seven a.m., she with five suitcases and a carry-on containing her camera and laptop. Harry had a single carry-on. His Miami flight left at nine-thirty, half an hour before Lucy's LA flight. They got their cell numbers and tentative plans to meet organized and said goodbye, Harry's hangdog, hungover face the unfortunate last image Lucy and the drugged and caged Claud had of him as he forlornly headed off to find his boarding gate. As he disappeared into the crowd charging through the terminal, Lucy found it hard to believe he was actually going to Florida to burrow a tunnel under the back end of a Wal-Mart in search of a plastic bag with a million dollars inside. She, on the other hand, had a contract and a check for eleven thousand dollars in her pocket, a one-month advance from the producers of the *X Dames*.

They had thrown in the extra thousand in moving expenses, and so after checking her bags, and dishing out a fifty-dollar tip to make sure Claud got treated right en route, and doing security, and hitting the latte stand, and grabbing a *Times* from the concourse newsstand, and waiting for half an hour at the gate, Lucy pre-boarded with the gilded gang, and traveled first class for the first time in her life. She was going Hollywood.

2

LA a-Go-Go

By the time the plane touched down at a little past one, LA's west-side morning marine layer had burned off, so Lucy got an eyeful of ocean as they glided into LAX. She badly needed that look at the Pacific—Southern California's great saving grace—to remind herself that she could actually stand the place for a few months. Especially after suffering through an extended overview, during her flight's approach, of the city's endless, smog-shrouded flats and valleys, where fifteen million or so people went about their daily business, almost all of them in cars. Every time she landed in LA, Lucy was appalled by the city's relentless suburbanization of every inch of land around the myriad mountain ranges that once hemmed it in. Even that sun-baked, forbidding desert terrain east of the San Fernando Valley appeared to be filling up with houses and cars and roads to carry them. But her sweet little soon-to-be home was down there, too, somewhere in the low-rise urban zone hugging the hazy shore between the two dinky piers of Venice and Santa Monica, just a few miles north of the airport.

By two o'clock, she had collected her bags and her still-dopey dog. She emerged from the baggage claim with a cart piled high, half-dragging Claud behind. Slipping on her shades, she headed for the curbside. The air felt perfect, around seventy degrees. New York was supposedly getting its first heat wave in the coming week. After waiting three anxious minutes, Lucy pulled out her cell and was just about to dial Terry's number when she spotted a bright orange VW bug convertible headed her way. Saved! She should have known. Terry was never late. And Hollywood jackpot or no, Terry was not about to give up on her sweet, funky old car. She'd bought it used in the late 1980s, and it had never once broken down. She pulled up with a wave and a honk, jerked on the parking brake, and jumped out. "Lucy Ripken, you are looking fabulous as usual!"

"Likewise," Lucy said. They met for a big hug, then stepped back for a better look. "Look at you, Teresa. Wow!" Lucy did a little double take. Teresa had long, shiny, dark red hair, wore low-slung jeans, and a short, navel-exposing T-shirt with a picture of Exene Cervenka on the front. She looked better than she had in years.

Teresa smiled. "Well, I never said I wasn't going to, you know—"

"You had some work done."

"A little. My eyelids were going south. And a chemical peel, for sun damage."

"You evil girl. You look twenty-five."

"What can I say? It's LA. Over thirty is over the hill around here."

Lucy held her by the shoulders and took a closer look. "Really, you look wonderful. Whoever it was did a great job." She paused. "Where do I sign up?"

"Lucy, many a time I heard you swear you would never do the dirty deed."

"That was then, this is now. No, seriously, I'm not in any rush. Hey, have you met Claud? Teresa MacDonald, meet Claud, the world's finest poodle." Terry reached down and patted him as Lucy went on. "He's still a little loaded from his dog dope. There's no way he would have gotten in that box without it. Claud, this is my pal Teresa."

The dog looked up, acknowledged her, then dropped his head. "Luce, you've got enough luggage for the grand tour. What's with all this?" Terry waved at the heap of suitcases.

"Harold convinced me to spring clean before I left. So I did, for the first time in, I think, seven years. I ended up getting rid of half my clothes. This is the other half."

"What, you're planning on staying here?" Teresa said. "You're no LA girl, Lucy. I wouldn't—"

"No, no, I just emptied out my place is all. I didn't even sublet it, so I must be planning on heading back sooner or later. Or turning bicoastal." She grinned. "Hey, I'm going Hollywood, right? I just might need to dress to impress."

"The only thing that impresses people around here are twenty-year-old girls with artificial breasts."

"It can't be that bad, Ter."

"Trust me. It is. The cosmetic surgery industry is taking over the world. Women are even getting their, you know, private parts done."

"Are you serious?" Lucy made a face. "God, that's bizarre."

"To say the least. But hey, it's LA, where insolent liquor store clerks card women as a come-on. And you know what? It works. Even on a dyed-in-the-acrylic cynic like me. Flattery will get you everywhere."

Lucy had another look at her, and grinned. "I don't know if I'd card you, but you could pass for twenty-fivish. Which ain't bad considering."

"That I'm four yards short of forty? Don't remind me."

"Hey, not to change the subject, but I don't know how we're ever going to fit all this stuff plus me and the dog in there," Lucy said, looking at the little car doubtfully.

"Cram, cram, cram, as my Scottish granny used to say about her garden," Teresa said blithely. "I've gotten really good at overloading this baby."

Ten minutes later, with suitcases piled high in the backseat, and sixty-five-pound Claud flopped in Lucy's lap, they drove out of the airport and north on Lincoln Boulevard.

"So where is Harold, anyway?" Terry asked a moment later, as they headed down from Westchester towards Marina del Rey.

Lucy surveyed the scene, one of rampant construction. "God, the last time I drove through here this was all open land."

"*Was* is the operative word. This close to the beach and marina, it was way too valuable to leave empty any longer. Once Hughes bailed out, it was just a matter of time."

"Right. Anyways, Harold's in Florida. I think he's gone completely crazy." Lucy gave her a shorthand version of Harold's tunnel scheme.

"Jesus, that does sound a little flaky. I thought he was a serious guy."

"He is, but—he's just tired of being broke, he says, and so—" Lucy shrugged.

"Well, I'm with him in that regard," Terry said. "I mean, if Bobby Schamberg had approached me even last year, I would have laughed in his face. But I, too, got sick of living in crummy apartments and only going out to dinner on somebody else's dime."

"I hear you. I just wish Harold had a better plan. Tunneling under a Wal-Mart just seems utterly insane to me. And I told him so. Hey, maybe you can hire him, too," Lucy said, only half-jokingly.

"I wish, but Bobby wants an all-woman—I should say all-girl—team." Terry honked. "Hey, move, moron," she yelled at a slow-moving silver Benz. "He's a total sleaze, Luce. Bobby, I mean. I did tell you that, right?"

"Yes, I guess you did. But his checks don't bounce, right?"

"No, they don't." Terry said. "You can take that eleven grand to the bank. In fact this is where I have my account." She pointed at a bank on the left, on one of the streets leading into the Marina. "You want to open an account now?"

"Later, later. I'd like to get to the new place, get the dog settled in, and unpack a little. OK by you?"

"Of course. I'm only two blocks away, Lucy. We'll be neighbors."

"Cool."

"So the thing about Bobby is he's really sexist in the crassest way, he'll talk about women totally in terms of their bodies, tits and ass, right to your face, but once he's decided he likes you and you're up to snuff in the brain department, he's completely loyal and reliable and a good friend. And he already respects you because of your book and because I told him he'd better or I'd walk."

"Oooh, you toughie."

"Hey, a girl's gotta do what a girl's gotta do."

After another five minutes of crawling up Lincoln through the thickest tangle of low-rent signage that Lucy had seen since Times Square cleaned up its act, they swung a left onto Breezeway Avenue. Two blocks later, Terry stopped the car in front of an anonymous-looking mint-green two-story apartment building on the south side of the street, with the number 637 written in 1960s-era script on the wall. "There it is, Luce," Teresa said. "Apartment 117, on the ground floor. Home, sweet home for the next however many months."

"637 Breezeway, Number 117," Lucy said. "Sounds pretty good."

"There's a nice little pool in the courtyard, no drug addicts or hookers, and the two grand a month gets you access to the laundry room as well," Terry said.

"Such a deal."

"Venice is very desirable."

"I thought you said it was two blocks from the beach," Lucy said. "This is more like six, right?"

"Sorry about that. The first place fell through. There was a rent-controlled tenant leaving after twenty-five years and at the last minute this girl paid him five grand to marry her so she could move in with him before he left, and take over the apartment. She's paying two hundred a month so she'll make her money back in saved rent in no time."

"God, it sounds like a real estate hustle right out of Manhattan."

"I guess. Hey, let's get your stuff inside. We should take turns with suitcases so we don't leave things unattended. After we unload I'll introduce you to the landlord."

"Landlord? He's on premises?"

"Yeah, he lives here. The owner/manager." She dropped her voice. "His ex is a friend of mine. That's how I found the place. He's like a fifty-year-old would-be artist, has two apartments here, one for his studio, one to live in. The work is ridiculous, these purple forest and rainbow paintings that look like—well, you'll see, since his studio is next door to your apartment. Plus he's got a twenty-year-old girlfriend. Younger than both his daughters."

"Ugh," said Lucy. "A dirty old middle-aged man."

"They're everywhere," Teresa said, as she grabbed a suitcase, went to the building's metal gate, and pushed a buzzer. "Fueled by Viagra and pornography, the aging dregs of the sexual revolution." She shook her head. "To get to your place, you turn right and head around the pool. You're in back on the right. I'll be back in a sec," she said, pushing open the gate when the buzzer sounded.

Lucy busied herself getting the stuff out of the car. Claud, emerging from his stupor, had a look around. The sunshine felt warm and soothing, the air carried a salty tang, and Lucy spotted two avocado trees and three orange trees within hailing distance. This was looking, well, not bad. Teresa swung the gate open. "Come on in, Luce, and check out your new pad." As Lucy swung by her, lugging a pair of suitcases, Terry dropped her voice and went on, "Mr. Manager—his name's Dan Hobgood—is at work in his studio. In a purple haze. His bimbo's by the pool."

Lucy turned right and followed a terrazzo breezeway alongside the building, with the pool hidden behind shrubbery and a second-story breezeway overhead. She turned at the corner, following alongside the building. To her left, she spotted a girl in an itsy-bitsy bikini bottom lying by the pool, a 1950s-vintage freeform beauty. The girl lay topless on her belly on a lounger, greased and roasting in the sun. Ahead, the sliding glass doors on two adjacent apartments were open. Out of one emerged a man of fifty who looked forty, barefoot in jeans and a T-shirt, with dyed white-blond hair and pale green eyes. "Hi, you must be Lucy Ripken. I'm Dan Hobgood. The manager. Let me help you with that." He took a suitcase. He was good-looking, tanned, well-built, five-ten, with a practiced, friendly smile that exposed perfect white teeth. He glanced poolside, then gave Lucy an appraising look. "Welcome to 637. Me and my three brothers own the place. And six other buildings in the neighborhood. I have two daughters that share an apartment upstairs. Mariah and Marcia. They're cool kids, but now and then they get a little partied up, but don't worry. They won't burn down the building or steal your shit. So your friend Teresa says you're planning to stay at least six months. That right?"

"I'm not sure. I've got a TV job, you know? They cancel the show—" she shrugged.

"Right, right," he said, nodding, still grinning. "The Industry. Well, you've got a six-month lease—or at least Schamberg Productions does."

"No problem." Lucy glanced into his apartment studio. Propped against the walls, the five paintings she could see were each four by six feet, and each worked the same motif: forests of luridly glowing yellow and purple trees beneath over-arching rainbows. A half-finished sixth occupied an easel in the middle of the room. "Intense colors there."

"You like 'em?" he asked. "I'm working on this gallery to give me a show, but so far it's like, if you aren't connected in the art scene nobody takes you seriously."

"Hey, I'm from New York, it's the same there," she said. "It's all about who you know." She smiled. "Well, I gotta get my stuff and get moved in."

"Right. Here's your place," he said, leading her to the next apartment. They entered through sliding glass doors. The living room was semi-furnished with a couch, chair, TV, and table, featureless but pleasant, well-lit by natural light reflecting off the pool and courtyard. The minimally equipped little kitchen was separated from a small dining area by a counter with a pair of stools. A door led to a bathroom, another to a bedroom. She lugged the suitcase into the bedroom. Another pair of sliding glass doors, a good-sized closet, a comfy-looking queen-size bed, a desk and chair. All in all, she thought—as she threw the suitcase on the bed and went back into the living room—not too shabby. Terry had done all right by her.

"You need anything let me know," Hobgood said, after handing over a set of keys and quickly walking her through the locks, switches, house rules, etc. "I'm two doors down, on the other side of my studio."

"Yeah, OK, thanks," Lucy said. He disappeared into the studio. Fifteen minutes later, she and Teresa had everything unloaded. They made a plan for the evening and Teresa drove off. Almost immediately the world's largest automobile pulled into the vacated parking space, with a pair of glam-looking, sunglasses-wearing girls in the front seat and a pair of surfboards sticking up out of the backseat. And so Lucy met Marcia and Mariah, Dan Hobgood's twenty-three- and twenty-one-year-old daughters, and their 1965 electric-blue Cadillac convertible, named Flash. They were both surfers, and the older one, Marcia, was a painter, "Just like my dad," she said with a smirk. "Only better," she added.

"Way better," her sister chimed in. They were both really cute, having expertly mined the endlessly trendy vein of surf-chick style for their mismatching hipster beach-babe looks—with a little Goth thrown in, in that both had dyed their long straight hair deep black. Lucy liked them immediately. "But then," Mariah lowered her voice, "Dad can't paint his way out of a sack."

"And everybody knows it but him," Marcia said. "It's kind of sad."

"I'll have to check out your work," Lucy said. "I know a couple of gallery people in New York."

"That would be awesome," Marcia said. "I'd love to get a show in New York."

So would just about every artist in the world, Lucy thought, but didn't say. The girl had no idea. "Come up anytime," Marcia went on. They got out of the car. "We're in 221."

"For sure," Lucy said.

She also met Alison, no last name offered, Dan's twenty-year-old girlfriend, who had perfect remodeled breasts, and had come from Scottsdale, Arizona, on a tennis scholarship to UCLA; only after a year she dropped out because she got offered a ten-second bit on a cable channel sitcom pilot, which launched her into her true calling. The ten seconds were axed before the pilot hit the air, and the show was axed the day after the pilot hit the air, but Alison was on her way to a storied Hollywood life. When Lucy told her that she was working as a writer on a new reality show called the *X Dames*, Alison went from friendly to fawning in a microsecond, sending Lucy scurrying into her new home. She closed the doors, drew the drapes, took a deep breath, and sat down on the couch, which smelled vaguely of salt and anonymous sexual sweat.

She pulled her cell phone out, wanting to call someone in New York, but there was no one in particular she wanted to talk to except Harold, whose warnings about LA life had begun to ring in her ears. Harold, however, was in Florida and had asked her not to call him for a couple of days because, as he had so pompously put it, he didn't want her to undermine his sense of belief in his mission.

So there was nothing to do but unpack, which she did for an hour. By then the time approached five. After briefly walking Claud around the neighborhood, Lucy jumped in the shower with a truly major question in mind: *what to wear* to her first *X Dames* meeting. Even if it was just a get-to-know-you dinner.

By six p.m., Lucy, in a little black dress, and Teresa, in a little red dress, had secured themselves a spot in one of the world's most scenic traffic jams, the one that migrated up the Pacific Coast Highway every weekday afternoon from three-thirty to six-thirty, between the last stretch of the Santa Monica Freeway and the Malibu Colony, several slow-moving miles to the north. They crawled along the edge of the Pacific, waves beating against golden sunset–hued sand a hundred yards to their left, stop-and-go creeping with the herd of wealthy strivers hauling their Bentleys and Porsches north to multimillion-dollar cribs on LA's Platinum Coast. Teresa held forth on the cultural scenery. Among the manses north of the Santa Monica Pier was Peter Lawford's, where JFK used to dally with assorted Hollywood babes procured by Lawford; and also the one where William Randolph Hearst kept Marion Davies prior to building his castle up at San Simeon. In not-so-rapid succession they passed Santa Monica Canyon; the prone-to-sliding cliffs edging the Pacific Palisades, where half the players in the Industry lived; the unglamorous terminus of glamorous Sunset Boulevard; Topanga Canyon, land of the ancient hippies; and finally, still short of Malibu, where the other half of the players lived, they turned right out of the crawl and within seconds plunged into unbuilt, unpopulated, preternaturally green Tuna Canyon. Soon they were car-climbing up the steep, sagebrush and sandstone slopes of the Santa Monica Mountains.

"So enough about movie stars and pretty scenery," Lucy said, waving at the hills and the oak trees and the deepening violet sky. The sun had set just as they turned off the

PCH. "What about you? Are you—you're not into something with this Bobby, are you?"

"Schamberg? God no," Teresa said. "He's fucking crazy. Not my type." She stopped short, and shot Lucy a pained look as they rounded another bend in the road.

"So—come on, Ter, what's the story?"

"You ever hear of a man named Paxton Whitehall?"

"Paxton Whitehall? No. Who is he, a member of the House of Lords?"

"No, no. I guess his name's kind of stuffy, isn't it? But no, he's just a guy who grew up in Oklahoma, then came out here years ago. A lot of years ago, actually. He was instrumental in getting the LA art world off its ass and into gear about forty years back."

"Teresa, how old is this guy?"

"He told me he was sixty-two but if he was, then he was already a successful art dealer when he was fifteen, according to the bio."

"So he's older?"

"I think seventy."

"You're dating a seventy-year-old guy?"

"I was. Then—" she slowed. "Check this view out," she said, pulling off at a turnout and stopping. They climbed out of the car and went to the edge. The whole of Santa Monica Bay, rimmed in lights from Malibu down to the tip of Palos Verde, stretched away before them. The dark silhouette of Catalina Island sat on the horizon.

"Wow, it's gorgeous," said Lucy. She turned and looked up towards the hills above them. "How much farther up's the house?"

"Oh, maybe five or six minutes," said Teresa. "Anyways, Luce, Paxton and I had an unusual relationship. I mean, it wasn't exactly like we were lovers, but we spent a lot of time together. Look, it was weird, okay? He had a thing for—he was always trying to get me to watch him have sex with young men. It was—"

"That sounds creepy, Teresa," Lucy said.

"I know, I know. But we had such a wonderful empathy, and I thought *that* part of his life was completely separate from the world he and I shared. Which was the art world, the cultural world, that he helped shape in Southern California for forty years. He was an amazing man, Lucy. An accomplished pianist, fluent in seven languages, profoundly educated in art history, a real Old World gentleman, from Tulsa, Oklahoma, of all the wiggy places, but still a complete and thorough-going Modernist, avant-gardist, totally in tune with what's up today. The perfect man, only—in any case, he finally talked me into, you know, watching. He said it was important to him. God knows why." She stopped. The silence was undermined by the white noise of the highway, a mile below them, and the warm breeze sighing through the sagebrush all around.

"So what happened?"

"I agreed to watch, and I did, and Pax had a stroke."

"While he was—"

"Yes. Humping this guy."

"Jesus. Did he—"

"Die? No. But the man—boy, really, he was only nineteen—kind of panicked and threw Pax off. Pax fell on the floor, and had some kind of seizure. I let the boy get dressed and run for it while I called 9-1-1. I didn't see any reason to—"

"So is he OK? Paxton, I mean."

"No, he got all fucked up. His brain was shot." She looked at Lucy. "I was in love with this old queen, Lucy, and I—I can't believe how stupid I was." Lucy had never seen Teresa even close to tears, but her eyes were shining now. "When the EMS guys showed up, I had to say that I was having sex with him when it happened, to cover for him since he was one of the last of the great closet queers—he'd been married for forty years till his wife died last year—but then they found some DNA that was neither mine nor his, and—let's just say it got really complicated really fast and then he had another stroke and died, and all the complications went away because his daughter got all the money. Unbeknownst to me, Paxton apparently had told her that he was going to change his will and put me in it in place of her. So she naturally felt kind of vindictive towards me. She had been the one pushing for this investigation, but all she really wanted was to make sure she got the money, and if she had to get me thrown in jail to accomplish that she was ready to do so. Since he hadn't changed the will yet, when he died she laid off, and the cops did too. They didn't give a fuck, really." She cried for a moment.

"God, that's awful, Teresa."

"So that's my love story for this year. Pretty sick, eh?"

"Doesn't sound like much fun, I have to say." Lucy managed a small smile.

"It was right after that I decided to take Bobby up on his *X Dames* offer. After all, Paxton and Milton Schamberg had been the best of friends.

"But that's way more than enough about me," Teresa said, suddenly resolute. "Let's get our butts up this mountain and see what our Bobby boy has to say, Lucy."

With that they jumped back into the car, and Teresa spun them around a few more hairpin turns, then abruptly whipped a left onto a dirt road marked with a bright blue mailbox sculpted into the shape of a breaking wave. As darkness fell, Teresa inched her way down the dirt road in first gear. Good idea: Lucy couldn't help but notice, on her right, about a foot from the edge of the road, meaning about two feet from the right front wheel of the car, the unfenced hillside fell away steeply down, down, at least five hundred feet down to the dark bottom of a dark canyon.

Thirty seconds later they swung around a small hill and there it was: with lights ablaze, what appeared to be a flying saucer from a 1960s science fiction movie, poised on the edge of the cliff overlooking a cosmically panoramic view of Santa Monica Bay and the Pacific Ocean and much of Los Angeles. A small fleet of pricey cars was parked by the saucer, and high hedges obscured assorted outdoor areas on both sides. "Oh my God," Lucy said, awestruck by the scene. She'd seen this house in magazines more than once, but the real thing was simply stunning, a vision straight from, well, a movie.

"Welcome to Moonship Mountain," Teresa said. "Where the rich got weird and the weird got rich."

"What do you mean?" Lucy said as they parked and got out of the car.

"Not much. It's really nothing more than another expensive and eccentric Malibu movie pad at this point," Teresa answered wistfully as they stood side-by-side, gazing at the spaceship. "With a stranger history than most. And of course one of the oddest architectural pedigrees you'll ever find. Milton's brother-in-law designed it. He was one of the original acid test participants, back when Ken Kesey and Tim Leary showed up with the first LSD. This was like 1965. He died young like his sister, certain that he was of alien origin. Or from the lost continent of Atlantis at least." She laughed sardonically. "Basically I just know way too much about what went on in this house back in the day." She reached out, took Lucy's hand, and squeezed it. "Thanks for asking about Paxton," she said softly. "I hadn't told a soul what happened until just now." The door flew open, and a figure draped in some sort of robe appeared in the doorway, a backlit silhouette. "Get ready for the song and dance, Luce. Looks like the Bobster's in full party mode."

Striding at them as they headed towards him, he emerged from backlighting and Lucy got a good look: circling fifty, broad handsome Mediterranean face with full lips and high cheekbones, wavy dark hair, small gold hoop earring on the left. Over a gym-fit six-foot-two-or-so body, he wore black pants, a white blousy shirt, and a black velvet robe that struck Lucy as a serious affectation. He looked as if he aspired to the style of a wealthy pirate. And had always been wealthy. "Hey Terry, so glad you could make it." He quickly shifted his attention to Lucy, with an intense once-over glance and a pair of actively flaring nostrils. Yes, I would fuck you if you'd let me, said the nostrils. She was supposed to be honored. She was not. "And you have to be the one-and-only Lucy Ripken." He took both her hands. "You look even better than Terry said you would." His dark eyes were intense, full of yearning—comic book yearning, Lucy decided. The guy was a clown. A perpetual adolescent. She knew the type.

"Hey, Bobby," she said. "I've heard a lot about you."

"Likewise," he said. "Only I've heard nothing but good and I'm sure you've heard nothing but bad."

"Bobby," Terry mock-whined. "I wouldn't bad-mouth you." She laughed.

"Yeah, right," he said, still holding Lucy's hands. "Other than to call me the number-one sexist pig in Hollywood, and a complete moron, and . . . "

"Hey, she's a big fan," Lucy said, firmly withdrawing her hands from his. "Let me assure you."

"Yeah, we both are," said Terry. "As long as you keep signing those checks."

"Har har har," said Bobby. "But seriously, Lucy, I did read your Mexican book, and I thought you spun a great story. Your skill at working a nonfiction story into a fiction-style narrative was impressive. That's why I was willing to let this here dame talk me into hiring you without a meet."

"Hey thanks," Lucy said, relenting. The guy gave good compliment. "I only wish the book was selling better, so that—"

"The *X Dames* takes off, I'll option it," he said. "And you can write the screenplay. That's a promise."

"Sounds good."

"Meanwhile, what's with the sorcerer costume, Bobby?" Terry asked as they headed towards the front door. "You're not throwing a séance tonight, are you?"

"No. As you know, that was my mom's game, and I never did like to play it. I was just—this was my dad's robe," he said. "And Judy—Judy's my ex-wife and current partner—it's a strange combo, I know," he said to Lucy. "But it works for us. Anyway, she was telling her surfer pal Henrietta—who's here tonight, and is going to compete in the *X Dames*, by the way—about Teresa and her book, and how my dad was such a sixties space cadet, so I got this old robe out to sort of illustrate. I mean, I remember my dad in this thing, long hair flying as he danced around the house. He and my mom." His eyes abruptly darkened. "Hey Jude," he said as a woman appeared in the doorway. "Terry's here, and she's got our new writer with her."

They stepped up onto the threshold. Terry said hello and went in, bound for the bar. Lucy and Judy shook hands, said hello, and instantly disliked each other. Lucy didn't know why, but the woman was off. Wrong. Dangerous. She was strikingly beautiful, in her indeterminate thirties, her perfect LA breasts well-displayed in a short, tight black dress. Stop looking at the tits, Lucy, she told herself. They all look like that! Judy also had long, strong legs and a firm butt, muscular arms, olive skin, a great tan, black hair—and the coldest, blackest eyes Lucy had ever seen. A first-class beach vampire if she'd ever seen one.

They all went in and did their introductory dances, and then the dinner went as such dinners go. Lucy found some stuff out about Judy Leggett and her friend Henrietta Walton, a small, pretty blonde woman with clear blue eyes that stared blankly, unblinking. She was in her late twenties, and served as Bobby's paramour of the moment, it seemed. She and Judy had passed back and forth the number-one American ranking in the women's pro surfing tour for seven years in the 1990s. Then Judy retired and Henrietta ruled until last year, when this Hawaiian girl Moki Sue Kalahana'I took over. Henrietta and Moki Sue, who Bobby described as an "Asian-American surf dominatrix," were both signed up for the *X Dames*, their fierce surfing rivalry a sure bet for on-set and on-show intrigue. At least that's the way Judy figured it, and had sold it to Bobby. Moki Sue was already in Mexico, sharpening her claws.

This particular predinner conversational minuet hit its climax when Judy smiled at Lucy, baring her gleaming fangs, and said, "But you already know your way around Mexico, right Lucy? I read that book you wrote about it."

"Did you? Cool," Lucy said. "I only wish more people had. I've made about five bucks off that . . . "

"In the book it seems like you really like to . . . stick your nose in places you shouldn't," Judy went on, still smiling.

Lucy picked up the vibe. "I guess I'm just a curious kind of girl," she said, eyes suddenly locked in a stare down with Judy.

"Curiosity," said Judy. "Now that's an interesting trait, don't you think?" She sipped at her sake. "Are you into the movies, Lucy?"

"Yeah, I mean I go, you know. . . . "

"I'm a film nut," Judy said. "Comes from being involved, I guess. Anyways, I was just thinking . . . Do you remember the scene in *Chinatown* that stars the director, Roman Polanski, Lucy?" Judy said. "You know *Chinatown*, with Jack . . . "

"Of course," Lucy said. "It's one of the great ones. I bet you're talking about the scene where Polanski plays a little gangster who sticks a knife in Nicholson's nostril as he threatens him."

"Exactly," Judy said. She reached out towards Lucy, as if holding a knife. "And Polanski's line was, 'You are a very nosy fellow, kitty kat.'" Judy smiled. "You know what happens to nosy fellows?" "And then he flicks it up," she said, flicking her invisible knife upwards, "and rips a slash in Jack's nose. And when Jack's bleeding, and reeling in shock, Polanski says, 'Wanna guess? No. OK? Lose their noses.'" She stopped, sipped her sake, smiled at Lucy. "It's perfect, don't you think?"

"Wow," Lucy said. "You've got a great memory for lines."

"I think I know that entire script by heart. Robert Towne wrote it. But I met Roman Polanski in Paris a few years ago," she said. "When I was just starting out on the surf circuit. There was a contest in Biarritz and we flew in through Paris. He's a sexy little guy, and I caught his eye." The smile abruptly left her face. "His last line in the scene, when Nicholson's about to collapse, goes like this: 'Next time you lose the whole thing, kitty cat. I'll cut it off and feed it to my goldfish, understand?' It was like, the perfect closer." She turned and walked away.

Dinner consisted of endless plates of freshly prepared sashimi and sushi. Two drop-dead-gorgeous female Japanese chefs in short, slit-to-the-hip silk dresses were on site in the thousand-square-foot designer kitchen at the center of the house, slicing and chopping furiously. The gang feasted at a large round table on a round patio set amidst sandstone boulders on the west side of the spaceship house. At the edge of the patio the land simply dropped away into darkness. Where Bobby's mother had fallen, or been pushed, many years back. They drank expensive sake by the quart and Japanese beer by the gallon. After a couple of trips to the head, Lucy figured out the floor plan: with long stretches of curving granite countertop open to the living and dining areas, the remodeled circular kitchen sat in the middle of the building, rooms arrayed around like wedges of pie, with dividing walls like wheel spokes. Situated on the west side, the living and dining spaces were vast, made vaster still by the ceiling that sloped down from a height of thirty feet over the kitchen to fifteen feet over the glass doors and walls framing the view. Stainless-steel rods placed at eight-foot intervals supported the concrete roof. The whole thing was a weirdly amazing piece of engineering and architecture.

They had a panoramic view of the bay and sea. They had fabulous food and drink. There were six women there counting the sushi chefs, and two men: Bobby and a big blond guy named Max, who served as driver, gardener, pool dude, and Judy-fucker, according to Terry. When not driving, gardening, doing the pool, or fucking Judy he stood in the shadows and didn't say a word.

Lucy found Bobby to be much as Terry described—a nice guy, sharp, funny, and even on occasion thoughtful, except that he was not only doing Henrietta but was also hot to trot with at least one sushi chef, judging by the way he pawed at her every time she delivered another perfectly sliced and organized platter of pink and red fish meat. She didn't seem to mind at all.

He slept with anybody he could con into his bed, Terry said, in a genial conversation that included the Bobster himself, as long as they had shapely tits and proved willing to blow him. He didn't disagree.

As the evening wound down, Lucy and Terry found themselves alone on the patio with double espressos to sober them up so that they wouldn't crash down the mountain driving home. At that moment, Lucy decided that nothing that had happened on her first day and night in LA had really surprised her, other than her visceral and seemingly reciprocated dislike for Judy Leggett, which had not lessened through the evening.

That was that. This was LA. And then as the two of them got up to leave they heard laughter and splashing and went to see what was up. Teresa led her through a doorway to another outdoor space, where a blue swimming pool shaped like a giant Egyptian scarab glowed, set amidst elegantly illuminated landscaping. In the beetle-shaped pool sloshed Bobby, Judy, Max, Henrietta, and both sushi chefs, all naked and ready for a promiscuous frolic. Bobby waved. "Coming in, girls?" he said.

"Yeah, right, Bobby," said Teresa, arms crossed. "Fat chance."

"OK, OK," he said. "So I'm a dirty old man. Don't forget the meeting tomorrow."

"Two p.m. at your office."

"Nice to meet you, Lucy," Judy said from the deep end, where she and her gardener were playing.

"Likewise," Lucy said. "Let's get out of here, Ter," she added under her breath. "I've got to walk my dog." And so they said thanks, goodbye, and took off.

"So that's the way it is, eh?" Lucy said once they'd gotten off the dirt road onto pavement, and Lucy felt safe enough to breathe. "They all end up in bed together."

"I guess," said Terry. "I've been here a couple of times, and by midnight it's always Bobby and whomever's willing in the pool. In this case, however, he's got himself a sure thing. I'm pretty sure those two chefs were more than sushi slashers. They were working girls."

"Hooker sushi chefs?"

"Hey, hot-shot sushi chefs are a dime a dozen in LA. As are beautiful young Japanese prostitutes. But you put the two together and you've nailed a niche in the market. Those two are savvy girls. They'll probably walk away tomorrow morning with a couple of grand apiece. Bobby is nothing if not generous."

"I see what you meant when you called him a sleaze. And not a bad guy at the same time."

"I know. He's a sexist creep, and yet he's so self-deprecating and self-aware, even though you know he's totally manipulative you still forgive him."

"What about the ex?"

"Judy? She's—I don't know, I've never really had a personal conversation with her."

"It was strange. She parlayed this little chat we had into an odd sort of threat. It was—oh, never mind," Lucy said.

"What?"

"I just got a bad hit off her."

"Aah, she's just another LA dame, Lucy. At her age—our age, actually—here in LA if you've ever been in what they all call the "Industry"—as if there is no other—you feel threatened all the time. By other women I mean. The ageism is just so intense. In truth I kind of admire her for being a surfing champion, you know? That's a really hard sport to get good at."

"Yeah, maybe I'm just jealous. Surfing's so much cooler than windsurfing these days, after all."

"Well, your windsurfing skills should help you figure it out fast. And from what I hear, Sayulita's a great spot to learn. The Wave Divas, a women's surfing school from San Diego, has been running a camp there for years. In fact, one of their instructors, this girl Sandra Darwin, is one of the *X Dames*. She lives in Sayulita and she's helping us put the show together. And competing. She's really cool."

"So we'll see her in a couple of days?"

"Yeah. In fact she's picking us up at the airport in Puerto Vallarta."

During dinner, Bobby had informed them that they were all leaving for Sayulita in two days, since most of the cast and crew were already down there, the surfing contest was set up for the upcoming weekend, and they needed Lucy and Teresa to write up some orchestrated sideshow confrontations between competitors, and possibly to do some casting of sexy Mexican and tourist extras as well as help with production logistics.

"Well, I guess I'll repack a bag," Lucy said half an hour later, as she and Teresa walked the quiet streets between their apartments, Claud off-leash frolicking ahead. For all its balmy, low-rise pleasantness, the neighborhood was not to be walked alone at night, Terry had said. A shadow could surprise you, jumping out from an unlit alleyway.

"Yeah," Teresa said. "Sorry you unpacked, but who knew?"

"It's cool. I love Mexico," Lucy said. "And I'm ready to roll into—whatever the heck we're going to be doing. But meanwhile, what about tomorrow?"

"I'll pick you up around ten, if it's OK. There's this old friend of Schamberg's I have to see in Pasadena, and I need backup. I've been trying to line up this interview for like two years, and the guy's a pain. I hear once you're in his house you're fair game." She paused. "Then you and I can grab lunch before the meet at Bobby's office."

"No problem. I'm gonna take an early beach walk—I haven't seen Venice Beach in years, so I need to do one before I cut out again—but I'll be back before ten."

3

Crosstown Cruising

At six a.m., Lucy got up with the early light, fed Claud a biscuit, then put on her speed-walking uniform—tennies, tight black shorts, and a midriff-baring, stretchy, form-fitting black-and-white top—and headed out. To a pleasant surprise: on the street in front of the building she and Claud discovered Marcia and Mariah Hobgood groggily loading surfboards, wetsuits, and towels into Flash the Cadillac. She said hey, and they said hey, wanna go surfing? She said, no but I'll take your picture. She ran back in to grab her digital camera, and a minute later she and Claud found themselves leaning against a pair of surfboards sticking up out of the backseat of a 1965 Cadillac convertible, headed to Bay Street, south of the Santa Monica Pier. Looking way cool in the rosy dawn, after a latte stop they cruised up Neilsen and cut over to the beach a few blocks below the pier.

In the nearly deserted beachfront parking lot, where a trio of scruffy teenage skater boys performed assorted board-flipping tricks, the girls wrapped in towels and transformed themselves from unkempt early morning hipsters into black rubber-suited surf seals. Lucy documented the transformation, and then documented the waxing of the boards. Mariah rode a six-foot-four-inch shortboard thruster sporting a red-and-black anime-style supergirl skateboard queen, while Marcia's classic nine-foot longboard noserider featured black-and-green snakes slithering intertwined up both sides in comic book Maya mode. Lucy captured the girls posing with their boards in the smog-softened pink dawn light, then she and Claud stood at water's edge to watch them paddle out. On this particular weekday morning, here at the edge of LA, the two sisters had this spot to themselves for the moment. A small miracle.

The set waves were shoulder- to head-high. With the sun rising behind her to illuminate them, and no marine layer to speak of, and a light offshore breeze blowing the wave edges back, the conditions approached perfection. This was LA at its best, Lucy thought, focusing her digital telephoto lens as Marcia snagged a head-high right-breaking wave, dropped in, and coolly shredded it with a series of classic, old-style bottom turns and cutbacks.

A minute later, Mariah paddled into a waist-high curl on her shortboard, and she, too, ripped her first wave, a backside left with a little tubular section maybe halfway down the line. Clearly they had both mastered the surf domain.

She watched for forty-five minutes, capturing a couple of dozen images, then speed-walked the beach with Claud, who happily chased gulls and shorebirds along the water's edge. By the time she'd done fifteen minutes south and fifteen minutes back, the girls were paddling in, ready to begin their day. And Lucy had a plan.

"You were great!" she shouted as the sisters walked in together, laughing it up as they talked over the day's waves.

"Hey thanks," said Marcia. "If I didn't get out here every day I think I'd go nuts. LA is so wacko."

"The surf is sweet today," Mariah said. "The offshores really set up the lines."

"Yeah," said Lucy. "I think I got some good shots of both of you."

"Cool," said Marcia. "Hey, you want to come back and check out my paintings now?" she added as they headed up to the car.

"Sure," Lucy said, checking the time. "What I'd really like to do is try a few waves but I don't have a wetsuit."

"You surf? You can borrow my stuff," said Marcia. "We look about the same size."

"Sounds good," said Lucy. "But I think I need a lesson. Maybe you can show me a few tricks."

"Anytime, Lucy," Marcia said. "Just knock on my door."

Lucy waited while they peeled out of their wetsuits and dressed. By the time they left the lot was half-full and about thirty surfers battled for the waves they'd had to themselves an hour earlier. Lucy read the journals: surfing had entered one of its periods of faddish popularity, when everybody all at once decided it was the cool thing to do. She knew from her windsurfing experience how fickle that scene was: once they all discovered how difficult it was to actually get good at surfing, most of them would be back on the sofa, watching it on TV. Watching the *X Dames*. Bobby had good timing. She opened up that line of conversation as they headed out of the parking lot. "So you girls know why I'm here, right? In LA, I mean."

"Dad said you had a gig on a TV show," said Marcia.

"Right," said Lucy. "But did he tell you what it's about?"

"No."

"It's called the *X Dames*." She thumbnailed it, then finished with a flourish. "And now let's cut to the chase: I think you girls should come down to Sayulita with me and get on the show and enter the contest. They're not done casting yet, and you'd be perfect. Young, cool, pretty, and great surfers. You're made for it. Both of you."

"Damn," said Mariah. "I can't just split school to—man, any other time I'd be there in a Malibu minute, but I've got three weeks left in this quarter. And I'm looking at a B average. I can't blow that."

"Where do I sign up?" said Marcia. "I've just finished a bunch of paintings, I'm like totally sick of my job, and I would love to go to Mexico."

"Plus she's like the best non-competing woman surfer in LA, I swear to God," said Mariah. "Besides me, of course."

"I kick your heinie all over the waves, Sis," laughed Marcia.

"No way."

"Way."

"Let me run it by my people," Lucy said, talking the talk. "But I'm pretty sure it'll work. I might even be able to swing you a ticket and a place to stay."

"That would be awesome," Marcia said as they pulled up to the building at 637. "So you still want to check out my paintings?"

"Absolutely," Lucy said.

Marcia's paintings showed great promise, Lucy thought. Portraits of her fellow waitresses, restaurant regulars, cooks, friends, and neighbors. The paintings were noirish, with hints of Hopper; somewhat derivative but infused, beneath the self-conscious bleakness, with a wonderful sense of LA light. She had the makings of a fine artist, potentially, but needed more training. "So why aren't you in art school?" Lucy asked, after telling Marcia what she thought. That the work was good but could be a lot better.

"Because I can't afford it and my dad didn't want to pay for it and so—" she shrugged. "I'm waitressing and painting in my spare time. And surfing, of course."

What a jerk, Lucy thought, recalling the four-by-six-foot pieces of self-indulgent junk she'd seen downstairs, and the six apartment buildings. The guy can't afford to send his daughter to art school?! "That's too bad. Well, listen, aside from the TV exposure, first prize in the *X Dames* is twenty-five grand for each round and a hundred grand for the grand finale, last I heard. So—"

"I win the contest I can afford to go to art school?" Marcia said. "That would be so awesome, Lucy!"

"I was thinking exactly the same thing," she said. "So why don't you check with your dad about going to Mexico?"

"Check with my dad? No way. He'll be like, you don't need to go to Mexico, you're just trying to avoid responsibility, you gotta pay your rent and car insurance and all that bullshit. No, I'm just going to go, Lucy. Mariah can tell him what's up."

"You have a passport?"

"Of course. And I'm twenty-three, so there's no stopping me."

Lucy ran it by Teresa en route to Pasadena. Teresa got Bobby on her cell phone, and after she described Marcia as a red-hot Goth artist surfer babe, he said fine, you and Lucy think she's hot, put her on the show. Just like that. Lucy called Marcia and told her to get packing, that a gofer would be in touch with flight information, and that they were off tomorrow. Marcia was unabashedly thrilled, which pleased Lucy no end.

Leaving smog-browned LA behind, they crested a freeway hill to find the hazy green borough of Pasadena spread out before them. "Thanks for doing that, Ter," Lucy said. "I know that girl's going to be a hot property, one way or another."

"Hey, I've known those girls since they were pint-sized. They're both great. I would have cast them as X-ers myself but I had no idea they surfed. Seriously I mean."

"They both kick ass in the waves. And Marcia's not a bad artist, either," said Lucy. "She'll be perfect for the show." She looked over the green sweep of Pasadena. "So refresh my memory on our next mission."

"Al DeLuca," Teresa said. "He's a dirty old demigod of the LA art world. He's been holed up in this falling-down Frank Lloyd Wright house for about nine hundred years, and supposedly he's got several of Milton Schamberg's early paintings in the garage, or basement, or somewhere. Plus he and Milton screwed many of the same Bohemian bimbos back in the day. He's a primary source, in other words, and I have been hounding him for an interview since I started this project. I don't know why he changed his mind—maybe he heard about Paxton and feels sorry for me—but in any case he finally returned my call last week, and we set this up.

"But all that background ain't shit. The real deal is that he's the last guy standing who was there the night Milton's wife died."

"The truth at last?"

"That's what I'm hoping. If I can get that maybe I can finish the damn book."

"So this is—"

"A major moment in my quest."

"I guess."

They got off the freeway, spent ten minutes going around in circles, and then found the place. On a quiet side street overlooking the Rose Bowl, it lay hidden behind massive walls of unkempt foliage, the only evidence of civilization being a broken-down Jaguar XKE parked out front with several parking tickets on the windshield. A man watering an immaculate lawn in front of an immaculate house across the street gave them the evil eye as they climbed out of the bug, sized the place up, and approached the rusted iron front gate.

From the gate they could see a house made of grimy gray-white cinderblocks, in a form that recalled a Mayan temple, buried behind layers of foliage on the other side of an unmowed thirty-foot stretch of crabgrass. Towering untended bougainvillea bushes threatened to devour the symmetrical building, its central portal framed by pilasters decorated with ziggurat patterns. "Chichen Itza goes Pasadena," said Lucy. "Even though it's a mess it's a cool building, don't you think?"

"Wright did several of these mocko-Mayan projects around LA," Teresa said. "This was one of the low-budget models." She rang a buzzer by the gate. They heard nothing. They waited. She rang it again. They sensed movement behind the bougainvillea. "There's the fabulous Al now," said Teresa, as the door opened and a scrawny old guy appeared in the doorway. He wore grubby cut-off jeans, flip-flops, nothing else. He hobbled three steps down off the entry porch and headed towards them.

"Who the hell are you?" he said. As he got closer they got a better look. Long, thin gray hair fringed a bald spot. His beard was ragged, his skin slack over a skeletal frame. He looked like a dirty old hippie man. His hands were stained with paint. Lucy could smell it. He was still working. Good for him.

"Teresa MacDonald, Al. And this is my friend—"

"Tomorrow. You said tomorrow," he said, arriving at the gate. He squinted through it at them.

"That was yesterday, Al. Which means I said today. At eleven a.m. Now it is five minutes past eleven. This is Lucy, my friend from New York."

"New York? What the hell you want to live in New York for? Bunch of backstabbing art critics and—oh, never mind," he went on. "I'm busy now. I'm working. Haven't worked in a while. But then when I decided to talk to you I thought I'd better make some new work so we'd have something to talk about besides all that crap from the 1960s. So I got inspired and I'm doing a new series now." He grinned slyly. "You're going to love the new work, ladies. Milton Schamberg eh? Ha! He always told me he'd give his right nut to be able to paint a figure like I can. The guy was an abstract expressionist because he couldn't figure out how to draw a goddamn thing."

"Hmmm," Terry said. "Well, anyways—"

"All right, all right," he said, fumbling with the gate. "You're here, so what the hell." He opened it. "Come in." They went in and followed him across the yard. He hobbled a bit, but not much, in fact for an eightysomething guy he was surprisingly spry, goatlike. "I'm not going to apologize for my house," he said as they ascended the steps. "It's been a mess for forty years so I figure why bother cleaning it now? Besides my maid quit a couple of weeks ago—she didn't like working around my paintings—and I haven't had time to find another one." They followed him into a large living room that smelled of fresh oil paint. DeLuca was hard at work—a half-finished piece sat on an easel in the middle of the room, next to a large table strewn with paint jars and cans of various sizes, along with palettes and brushes. The room was lit with cheap spots in metal shades, clipped onto window frames and curtain rods and chair backs and everything else. Plants had grown over the windows outside, rendering the room fairly dark, but the spots threw bright hot light on the paintings that leaned against walls, easels, and chairs.

One look and they knew why the maid had quit. Like Dan Hobgood—only Al DeLuca was a far more accomplished painter—Al DeLuca had a single subject for every painting, at least in this current series. And that subject was the private parts of the female anatomy, rendered in warm, rich color and realistic detail on a huge scale.

There they stood, the two women in their thirties and the ancient artist, surrounded by his huge, colorful paintings of female genitalia. Vaginas. Pussies. Cunts. Twats. Kukas. Petaled like flowers, sculpturally shaved or naturally furred, decorated here and there with delicately jeweled rings or tiny silver posts, in sizes ranging from a square foot to six by six feet, realistically rendered, they filled the room.

Every one of them possessed an undeniable beauty, in their layered, flowery, individualized way, Lucy thought, but kept quiet. This was Teresa's party. But Lucy knew this: whatever else you wanted to say about him, he worships what he's painting, blasphemously intimate or not. An artist named Judy Chicago had already covered this territory in intensely rich detail several decades back, but you know, Lucy figured, landscapes have been done by hundreds of painters, as have portraits. In the age of tell-all and show-all, why not this?

Teresa looked at him deadpan. "So who are your models, Al?" she said.

He gestured at a stack of magazines on a table otherwise strewn with empty take-out food containers. "Pornography provides all the imagery I need," he said. "They turn women into trash, and I turn them back into art."

"Interesting," said Teresa. "I wonder who'll show them?"

"I don't give a good goddamn who shows them," DeLuca said. "I'm painting for myself, and for posterity."

"Right on," said Teresa. "But I wonder if—I don't think I can do an interview in here, Al. These paintings are way too distracting. Would you mind if we moved to another room?"

"If you promise to model for me. Both of you," he said, then cracked up. "Just kidding, ladies. Yes yes, let's go in the kitchen. I know you're interested in seeing my Schambergs so I set them up in there."

They followed him through a doorway into the kitchen, a tiny, dark, cluttered space that reeked of stale tobacco smoke. "That so-called genius Frank Lloyd Wright didn't know shit about how people actually live," DeLuca gestured at a table built in to the far wall. "This kitchen sucks." A pair of foot square paintings sat on top, resting against the wall. He turned on the lights. Fluorescents sputtered to life, turning everything a pale shade of green.

"Ah," said Terry. "The Schambergs." She went over. Lucy followed. The twinned paintings were small, abstract, dark things, not particularly interesting. "These would have been from his Chicago days, right? Before he moved out west?"

"Hell if I know," DeLuca said. "We did a trade one time, probably early sixties, when we were drunk. I think I gave him a drawing of a dog I did."

"Actually it was a cat. I saw it," Terry said. "His son's still got it up at the spaceship." Terry made some notes in a small binder she'd conjured up out of a pocket. Lucy recalled seeing a cat drawing in the bathroom at the flying saucer house. It hung on the wall over the guest bathroom toilet, so guys could look at it while they peed. A place of dubious distinction, she thought.

"That's all fine and dandy," said DeLuca. "So you've seen the great Schambergs," he said dismissively of the paintings. "But that's not really why you're here, is it?" He sat at the table, laid the two paintings face down, and lit a cigarette. "Hey, I'm eighty-four years old and I've been smoking for sixty years. So don't even start."

"No problem, Al," Teresa said.

"Good. So what then?"

"Yes, you're right," Terry said, sitting across from DeLuca. Lucy stood close to the door, but there was no escaping the smoke. "What I'm really interested in is—"

"The night Milton's wife died," he finished for her. "The notorious night of Sheila's demise. That's why you're here." He smirked. "Yes, I was there, and yes, I saw it happen." He stopped, sucked on his cigarette, coughed up a gob, and spit it into a dirty dishtowel. "It was 1965, '66," he went on. "I can't recall exactly, but Sheila's brother Ronnie knew Ken Kesey because he'd gone to school with him at Stanford. Kesey showed up with that gang of fuckups, the Merry Pranksters, and the next thing we all knew Ronnie had a handful of acid tabs. LSD. Whoo-hoo!" he cackled. "The first goddamned LSD in Southern California, manufactured by the notorious Owsley himself, we were told. We didn't know what the hell it was so we started taking it and man, our brains were fried. I mean who knew! It was madness up there. The flying saucer—while he was building it we really thought it was a spaceship half the time, and that we all came from another planet to land on earth and would be returning soon. What a scene. Everybody naked, that little kid Bobby charging around—that kid saw everything, I tell you—and these guys from the Byrds and Love and the Mothers of Invention and all these bands were around, jamming. So." He stopped, flipped over a Schamberg, and proceeded to put his cigarette out right in the middle of it. "So much for that piece of shit," he said, smirking. "I've been wanting to do that for about thirty years." The pungent smell of burning oil paint layered itself onto the tobacco reek.

"Jesus, Al, you didn't have to—"

"Don't go telling me what to do, young lady," he interrupted Teresa. "You can see as well as I can that the painting's a piece of crap."

"But it's historically significant, Al. You know that Milton's reputation is going to be salvaged by my book."

"I'll be dead by the time your goddamn book comes out, young lady." He lit another cigarette, coughed, and laughed. "I've got lung cancer. What do you know! Hahaha."

"I see," said Terry. "So you're burning bridges since there's no point in—"

"No point in anything, except painting pussy," he cackled, then straightened up, dragged on his smoke, and went on. "We were all eating acid like candy, and then one day right around sunset Milton says to Sheila, I can fly, and she says, so can I, so they stood on the edge of the deck together, joined hands—me and about six other people were sitting around completely stoned, watching them as if they were—what?" His face grew dark. "I don't know, but the next thing we all knew, they were holding hands and getting ready to jump, bending their knees together, and then—Milton let go just as she jumped, and she tumbled three hundred feet, where she bounced off a big rock and then fell another hundred feet. Milton just stood there, staring down. Finally he said, Oh My God I didn't really think she was—I never intended. I was the first over to his side, and I looked down and saw this little crumpled body way the hell down there. I looked at Milton, and in his eyes I saw—" He sucked on his smoke, coughed, and stopped, waiting for a cue.

"What did you see in his eyes?" Terry said softly.

"That he had planned the whole thing. Or at least orchestrated it. Stoned as he was and I was, I knew in that instant that he was a killer. And that he'd gotten sick of Sheila and didn't want her around." He dragged on his cigarette again, and blew the smoke out.

"So he didn't push her but he—"

"Made it happen," DeLuca said. "I split before the cops showed up, because I didn't want to have to explain what I saw to them. Not in the state I was in. But everybody there covered Milton's ass because they didn't want the party to end.

"And you know what?" he added dramatically. "I never saw Milton again after that day. Didn't go to his funeral, which was a couple of years later—he managed to kill himself with drugs, too," he added. "His so-called heart attack was speed or cocaine at work, no doubt about it." He slid out from his seat at the table, creakily stood, and said,

"So there you have it, ladies. Maybe you can finish your goddamn book now, and start another one on something more worthy. Like my goddamned career, since I could always paint circles around that son of a bitch."

They all went back into the living room, where the spots still glowed on the paintings. "Look at these," said DeLuca. "Compare them to that shit in the kitchen."

"Thanks for your time, Al," Teresa said quietly. She looked at her watch. "But we've got a meeting."

"So go, goddammit, go," he snapped. "Get the hell out of my house." Lucy opened the front door and sucked in some fresh air. Teresa joined her a few seconds later. The door slammed behind her.

"What a cranky old lunatic," Lucy said.

"No shit," Teresa said. "But I got my story, didn't I? Admittedly it was kind of anti-climactic, but I'm certain that writing up this particular encounter will be quite amusing. And I can write it so that it feels like it mattered, know what I mean? The jump/push murder/suicide, whatever it was." She sighed. "In spite of what he says I don't think Al really knows what happened that day. But ambiguity has its own charms, I think." She paused. "In any case I gotta move forward or I'll never get the damned book done. So let's get out of here."

Five minutes later they were on the freeway. After a burger stop at Teresa's favorite lunch joint, the Pantry in downtown LA, they headed back to the west side.

Schamberg Productions was located in Mar Vista, in a renovated low-rise factory complex that once upon a time housed half a dozen manufacturers of assorted mechanical tools, toys, and trinkets, now made in China for far less. The renovation had turned the site into a low-budget architectural showcase, all cheap clever materials and crazy angles, bright colors and twisted finishes, deconstructed modernism at its computer-aided best. The compound was, as Teresa put it, "infested" with film and television production companies. She maneuvered the orange bug amongst the buildings and parked outside one. A loading dock reached via a hot pink metal stair provided access. They went in, sat for thirty seconds in a waiting room furnished with chairs made of layered cardboard, then got ushered in by a Schamberg minion who appeared to have waltzed off the pages of *Playboy*. Another pair of perfect breasts led the way.

The meeting took place around a conference table in Bobby's office. In attendance with Teresa, Lucy, Bobby, Judy, and Henrietta were a couple of executive producers, two handsome boys with expensive bad haircuts called Billie North and Sam Kane, both chronologically under thirty and mentally under twenty. They wore unmatched but exactly similar outfits: precisely distressed two-hundred-dollar jeans and T-shirts with retro commercial logos. They were dismissive of everybody except Bobby, who wrote the checks, and the director, a woman of forty or so named Mary Miles who showed up five minutes after Teresa and Lucy. Mary had short black hair and dark eyes. She had directed several successful segments on two of the most popular reality shows in the last five years, so her rep was immaculate. Lucy took to her immediately, possibly because she seemed to have a normal female body with a few normal years showing on it, and on her face, weathered from shooting outdoors in tropical climates. She would be directing the Sayulita sequence, one that Bobby said he hoped would run for the first two weeks, or otherwise serve as a two-hour Reality Movie of the Week pilot, which he figured to make a major splash in the fall sweeps—although the boy EPs both urged a late summer debut, when everything else on TV was dead in the water. Unable to chime in as they were not in attendance at the meeting were two other producers, Sophie Greenberg and her partner, a Mexican-American money man named Ruben Dario. Sophie was on the road with a location scout, searching out a mountain for the snowboarding segment. Dario, who owned a substantial piece of Schamberg Productions as well as a realty business and several houses in Sayulita, had already taken a crew and headed down to set up the surfing contest. Judy Leggett had used her surfing connections to hire a wavetracker plugged into the Pacific storm grid, and she reported that all signs pointed to a major west swell banging into Sayulita by the end of the week.

Finally at a certain point nearly an hour into the meeting, when all the egos had been properly massaged, Teresa said, "Hey, Bobby, this is all very nice and I'm really glad we're heading down for the shoot and the waves are coming, but—" She looked at Lucy. "Well, you've hired me and this other hot-shot writer, Ms. Lucy Ripken here, and we are heading down there to 'write' exactly what? I guess we should somehow know this by now, possibly by some sort of osmosis, but—" she shrugged.

A silence fell on the room as all eyes turned to He Who Signs The Checks, Bobby. He looked to the director. "Mary?" She smiled at Teresa and Lucy, completely relaxed.

"Hey, not to worry," she said. "Last time I did one of these, the writers—I guess that's what you called them—pretty much just put people in a room, or on a beach, or around a campfire, this would be after they spent some time with them so they kind of knew where they were coming from. And they said, OK, you're the schemer, you're the ditzy dame, you're the gentle but profound soul, you're the macho mama, you're the dynamic babe, and so on. They'd write a few starter lines of dialogue for different scenes, suggest possibilities for conflict and narrative, tell them just be yourself only more so, and then get out of the way. Since they're all young and hungry one way or another, theoretically the potential twenty-five or a hundred grand and the possibility of major air time will stimulate their cute little asses into doing some dramatic stuff, right? Plus the surfing contest is for real, we've got a couple of hotshot surfers to be judges. We'll take the top finishers from there, round up more contestants, and move on to what's next, right, Bobby?"

"That's right," Bobby said. "So any problem with that?"

Lucy and Teresa exchanged glances. "Nope," Teresa said. "Piece of cake. Right, Luce?"

"Can of corn, Ter," Lucy said, thinking, hundreds of thousands of dollars are riding on this? "So we have Henrietta here, and Moki Sue and Sandra Darwin already down there, and my young friend Marcia Hobgood coming down with us *mañana*. That makes four. Who else is going to compete in this segment? Do you have any, you know, pictures, profiles of the contestants, anything like that?"

"We've lined up a couple of competitive surfers from LA and San Diego, and several Mexican women's surfing champions to make the locals happy and to keep it—culturally diverse. And of course we have to round up a couple of—ringers, I guess you'd call them," Judy said. "Women who are surfers—well, look like surfers, anyways—but they've got, you know, the look."

"Yeah right," said Teresa. "That would be the 'enhanced' look?"

"It's the twenty-first century, Teresa. People can look the way they want to, and people on TV, especially, have to look a certain way," Judy said, crossing her arms beneath her own shaped-to-perfection, well-displayed breasts.

"She's absolutely right," Bobby said. "You shoot TV with babes on a beach, you gotta throw in some well-filled sexy bathing suits. That's *de rigueur.*"

"So you have maybe ten or twelve women to compete, a tropical location, a crew, and a plan. Sounds doable." Lucy got up. "Well, I've got to get back to my hacienda and get organized. I just arrived from New York yesterday, and I am scattered as hell." Teresa stood. "So I guess I'll see you all down in Sayulita."

"Cool," said Bobby. "Yeah, we're going down tonight so we'll have you all set up at the Villa Roma. Got a suite for the three of you. You two and the Hobgood babe."

"A suite?" Terry said. "You mean we don't get private rooms?"

"There weren't enough available," Bobby said. "But don't worry. Sandra says the Villa suites are fine."

"I'll be all over the Internet tonight to make sure," Teresa said. "And if they're not you have a problem. In fact you have three." With that she waltzed out, Lucy right behind her. They waited until they got outside. Then Teresa said, "God, no wonder I never did this Hollywood shuffle before."

"Hey, it wasn't so bad, Ter," Lucy said.

"You're right. Just jerks jerking off. And I like the director. Seems like a no-bullshit gal. But the main thing is we're off to Mexico tomorrow and they're paying us."

"A lot of money."

"Yes," said Terry. They got in the car and headed out of the complex. "I'm making more money this year than I have in the last five put together. All because of this ridiculous TV show."

"Likewise," Lucy said. "Sayulita here we come."

4

Surf and Turf in Sayulita

With luggage in hand and a pair of surfboards in silver bags racked on the roof, Lucy, Teresa, and Marcia shared a cab to the airport early the next morning. They did the airport shuffle, boarded, and eventually took off. Marcia promptly passed out with her head glued to the window, leaving Teresa and Lucy to contemplate their young companion. "She looks a little wasted," Terry said quietly.

"I know," Lucy answered. "When I went to get her she was still unconscious. As was her sister. As were the two dudes with them." She stopped. "It took me five minutes to shake her awake, and the boyfriend or whoever he was did not appear to be a happy little surf-puppy."

"What do you mean?" Teresa asked.

"There was some strange-looking paraphernalia on the stove and table," Lucy said. "I don't know the drug of choice these days but this looked like some demented child's chemistry set."

"Speed, I'll bet," said Teresa. "A lot of people are into it because it's cheap and easy to make, and they say the rush is better than cocaine and lasts for days." She looked grimly amused. "And best of all it destroys your brain faster than any other drug."

"Jesus," Lucy said. "What have I gotten us into? And my poor dog, for that matter. Marcia's sister said she'd take care of him while I'm gone."

"He'll be OK. They wouldn't have been passed out if they were on a speed binge. Plus if they're surfing every day they can't be doing it that much. Your body just can't take it. In any case, if speed's Marcia's demon of choice she probably won't be able to get any down there. The whole concept of speed is completely anti-Mexican. She'll have to dry out."

"Hope you're right," Lucy said. She sighed. "At least I didn't see any syringes."

"Yeah. It's not like we're going to have time to babysit a fucked-up twenty-three-year-old with a drug issue. We got TV to write, right?"

"Right," said Lucy, happy to change the subject. "So that meeting was all well and good, but do you really know what we're going to do?"

"You've seen reality TV, right, Lucy?" She looked at her. Lucy looked back solemnly, then burst out laughing.

"Actually I did watch *Survivor* once," she said. "And I saw *American Idol* when I was at my friend's house one time."

"That's it?" Teresa asked, grinning. "Well, that means you've watched about two hours more reality TV than I have, Lucy. Bobby never even thought to ask, so intent was he on hiring me—us—but the truth is, I don't even have a television."

"I'd say that if we weren't such literary geniuses we'd be in deep shit, Ter," Lucy said. "But knowing that we are, in fact, obscure but authentic literary geniuses, we will simply create a masterwork of televisable reality. Out there amidst *las olas altas.*"

"No doubt, Chiquita," Teresa answered. "Or get fired and go home." Marcia stirred. "The dead live again," Teresa exclaimed. "Stand back." The girl shuddered, then went back to slack-jawed sleep. Now that she had a chance for an extended, up close look at Marcia, Lucy didn't like what she saw. A sallow sickliness suffused her skin. Her eyes wore raccoon rings. She looked worn way beyond twenty-three years.

But on the other hand, the girl was smart, sexy-cute, and a hot surfer. Lucy knew her own enthusiasm had gotten her into this situation. She'd fallen for Marcia's sense of style, in her flash car, on the beach, in the waves.

Lucy shook her worries off. "So tell me everything else you can think of about what we're going to do with the show, Ter," Lucy said.

"Well, to begin with, I think we've got to get some serious conflict going ASAP," Terry said, whipping out a notebook. "Let's take a meeting, Lucita." They spent a couple of hours scheming *X Dames* plotlines involving shark attacks, Mexican-flavored beach parties leading to tequila-drunken catfights, collisions in the waves, international romantic intrigues, offshore diving adventures gone wrong, weird encounters with enchiladas, and other potential narrative thrills. Though it was tempting, they entertained and then dropped the idea of having Marcia's apparent drug problems enter into the story. By the time they were closing in on Vallarta they had several pages of dramatically enhanced reality mapped out around the surfing contest. And then with a swoop over the Bay of Banderas and a semicircular maneuver to approach from over the valley to the east, they landed with a single bounce—just enough to shake Marcia awake—followed by a smooth glide down the runway.

Twenty minutes later they found Sandra Darwin, a six-foot-two-inch Amazon of a surfer girl, waiting amidst the gang of sign-waving hotel limo drivers and timeshare hustlers and other airport scammers outside customs. Sandra held a sign with Teresa's name on it. Upon seeing her, Lucy named her the girl from Ipalita, cousin to the girl from Ipanema, for she was definitely tall and tan and young and lovely, except that at twenty-seven years old Sandra Darwin was way too cut to be an entirely convincing bikini beach babe from Brazil or anywhere else. She wore shorts and a tank top and flip-flops, and had hard, ropy arms and legs. Though her blonde-banged, blue-eyed face was pretty enough, she didn't sport much in the way of curves, real or fake, in the usual places. What she sported was sinew and muscle. She looked like she could kick ass. "Hey girls," she'd asked when they approached, dragging boards and suitcases. "Who's the surfer?"

"Me," said a groggy Marcia. "I'm—"

"I'm gonna whip your booty in the contest, honey," Sandra said, and then laughed. "Just kidding, kid."

"Hey Sandra, how are you?" Terry said.

"You're Teresa?" she asked.

"Yeah. Call me Terry. Or just Ter. Nice to meet in person at last, after all the email. And this is Lucy Ripken, and Marcia Hobgood, your competition."

"Hey," said Lucy. "How's it going?"

"You're the hotshot windsurfer, right?" said Sandra. "Did the Precolombian fake book?"

"Yes, that's me. I get around out there," Lucy said. "But I'm not—"

"I liked that book. Read it in a night. Let's blow this joint," Sandra said. "I hate airports." She was an abrupt one, or maybe just a non-bullshitter. Nothing wrong with that, Lucy decided as they followed her out to a tank-sized white SUV, strapped the boards on the roof rack, and threw everything else in the back. They soon found themselves headed north on the coastal road.

"Beer and sodas in the cooler there. Help yourselves," Sandra said a moment later into the rearview. Lucy handed Terry a ginger ale and opened one herself.

Marcia cracked a Tecate, took a half-can swig, and said, "Aaah. I needed that."

"I guess you did," said Lucy, giving her a look. She gazed back inscrutably, her eyes circled by darkness, until Lucy looked away. "Hey Sandra, how long's the ride?"

"Half an hour unless we get stuck behind a slow truck. The road gets pretty skinny and curvy once you get past the Punta di Mita turnoff." With mountains rising beyond a hazy valley to the east, and the Pacific to the west, they drove north through a landscape of scattered development, a classic colonized Mexican mingling of raggedy-ass little towns and ramshackle roadside retail buildings and over-sized bilingual billboards touting everything from Kahlúa to Hummers, interspersed with new golf courses, condo developments, hulking overscale hotels and timeshares along the shoreline to the west, and herds of horn-honking cars, trucks, buses, and motorcycles jockeying for position on the four-lane road. For fifteen minutes, Sandra pointed out the sights and named the towns and turnoffs—Nuevo Vallarta, Mezcal, Bucerias, La Cruz di Huanacatle, Punta di Mita—as they cruised along, paralleling the windy blue seas of Banderas Bay. Then they went through a checkpoint manned by a uniformed squad of what appeared to be sullen teenagers hefting submachine guns—*Federales,* Sandra said—and followed the light flow of traffic as two lanes on each side shrank to one and the road snaked into jungle-covered, hilly terrain.

Fifteen twisty minutes later they hit a flat, open stretch, where Sandra whipped a left turn onto a newly paved road. "They just did this road," she said. "Used to be a potholed mess, back in the good old days," she sighed. "But now—"

"What?" Teresa said.

"You've never been here, right? None of you?"

"I only go to New York," Terry said. "This is my first time out of the U.S.A."

"I was in Mazatlán once," Lucy said. "In college. Drunk for a week. And I've tripped through the Yucatán a few times, but that's another world over there."

"I went to Ensenada last year with some friends," Marcia said. "We partied, and surfed, and partied and surfed some more, and then went home. It was cool."

"Well, Sayulita *was* really cool," Sandra said, as they turned right off new asphalt onto a dusty, semi-paved road, and slowed to dodge several potholes. "It used to be the perfect little Mexican beach town, but unfortunately it's just too damn close to the PV aeropuerto. Which means that in the last two or three years it has gotten overrun with gringos of a different persuasion than the surfers, artists, and nomadic hippies that have always come here. Now there's a bunch of old fart Republican types building houses on the hills and—don't get me wrong, there have always been a lot of Americans down here, and Canadians, and even some Euros, because it is a really cool town, with a nice beach, good fishing, and a fun surfing wave. But now the development is happening way too fast, and the fun and funky vibe is less fun and funky it seems like every year."

"Money does that," said Lucy.

"Everywhere and always," said Teresa.

"Yeah, I know," Sandra said. "But I came down here seven years ago to surf and hang out, and then I got the Mexican branch of the Wave Divas off the ground and I never thought about buying property, even though it was still pretty cheap four or five years back. And now all of a sudden everything is for sale, but without serious hustling and hassling buying anything is practically impossible. That's why I gotta kick your booty in the contest, Marcia," she said, and laughed mirthlessly. "I could use that *X Dames* dough. So if you turn here," she said as she slowed and pointed to the right, "and go down there to the end of that dirt road and turn right on the beach road, you're headed into the north end, where the rich gringos are building their trophy haciendas on the hilltops. Downtown's across the bridge just ahead. Along here you've got your roasted chicken stand, your paint store, your hardware store, hair salon, glass art gallery—" They approached the bridge, and eased over. The river was a brown trickle flanked by mud banks. Beyond the downtown ahead they could see dozens of white Mediterranean-style houses scattered across the hillsides; between the established houses, half-built projects occupied much of the open land. "The river's kind of scuzzy—a lot of sewage still goes in untreated, unfortunately, but the Mexicans have always done it that way, and when there were only a few hundred of them it didn't hardly matter. Now there's a few thousand Mexicans and gringos, and their shit stinks.

"But what the hell," she went on, as they cranked a right. Ramshackle stalls housing craft vendors and food shops and plastic toys and kitchenware lined the riverbank on their right. "There's a great swell right now and the surf is way large for Sayu, so the contest should be intense. Fantastic timing for the show." She looked back at Marcia. "Are you ready, kid?"

"May I quote you?" said Marcia. "I'm gonna whip your booty."

Sandra laughed. "We'll see about that." She turned left onto a dusty street lined with parked cars in front of small stores and houses behind foliage-covered walls. She drove two blocks, turned left again, and parked. "Here we are, girls: beautiful downtown Sayulita. The town plaza's right there." She pointed straight ahead. "Everybody hangs out there in the evenings. The beach is behind us one block.

You're supposed to meet Ruben Dario, one of the *X Dames* producers, at El Costeño, the open-air restaurant on the beach at the end of the street. I should warn you: some think Ruben's the big bad wolf in this town, and he knows it. But the waves are right in front so you can check it out. I'll take your stuff to the VR—it's down the beach, you can't miss it—and catch you later."

"Cool," said Lucy, climbing out. "The air's nice here," she said.

"It's usually eighties by day, high sixties by night, until June. Then it gets stinky hot and sticky. Anyways you're also scheduled to meet Bobby Schamberg and Judy and that whole gang at Bobby's rental house, La Casa de la Luna Grande, on the beach at the north end of town, at seven o'clock for dinner. It's about a half an hour's walk from the hotel, or you can have them get you a taxi. Your stuff'll be in your suite. See you then," Sandra said. She drove off.

"Well here we are," said Lucy, taking a look around. "Looks like a sweet little town." Mexican and American hippies and surfers of all ages, girls in bikinis, sun-baked families, excited kids, barking and scrounging mongrel dogs, and dusty vehicles crowded the streets. Everything moved at a tropical crawl. It smelled of dogshit, fried fish, sunscreen, spilled beer, and the sea.

"Let's go check out the waves," said Marcia. "I gotta see what the surf's like."

They walked down the middle of the dusty street, lined with two- and three-story buildings, ground-floor tourist shops selling Mexican art, surfboards, bottled water, beer, clothes, groceries, and, in at least four different storefronts,

REAL ESTATE. "She wasn't kidding about the development, was she?" Lucy said. "It's Realtor hell."

"I heard it's because gringos can buy waterfront now without having a Mexican partner," Teresa said. "You can get some kind of bank trust. Used to be foreigners couldn't buy within a thousand meters of the beach. But now—" she shrugged.

"Holy shit, look at that surf," Marcia said, speeding up, grogginess magically gone as the waves beckoned. Past a row of craft vendors' tables set up on the sidewalk at the end of the block, and the beach beyond, they could see the ocean: white water everywhere, waves crashing across the bay, a rocky point with a huge house atop it a quarter of a mile away to the southwest, and a couple of dozen surfers spread out from the crowded beach before them to the outer lineup, maybe two hundred yards off the shoreline. They hit the beach. El Costeño was on the right, its expansive palm thatch roof shading rows of mismatched grubby white wood and plastic tables and chairs sitting in the sand. To the left a large temporary pavilion had been erected atop a framework supported by metal poles buried in the sand, with *X DAMES* emblazoned in bold blue letters across the four sides of the pyramid-shaped white fabric roof. Parked directly behind it was a four-wheel-drive truck, its canopied cargo bed loaded with video gear. A bored-looking guard stood by, in the shade of an elevated platform that had been put up for the surfing contest judges and perhaps a cameraman. "I gotta get my board and ride some waves," Marcia said. "The surf looks awesome. Where did she say the hotel was?"

"There," Lucy said, pointing. "It's that hulking monster." A quarter of a mile down the beach, where the road curved seawards towards the house on the point, a six-story building rose up in front of a small hill blanketed with white, red-roofed houses buried in flowering foliage and coconut trees. The top story appeared unfinished, all raw concrete, empty windows, and scraggly rebar. Several of the lower floors looked half-done as well. On the hill around it, the smaller buildings blended into the greenery.

"That's the Villa Roma," said Teresa. "I checked the site out on the Web last night. And also several other Sayulita sites and blogs. Seems that everybody in town hates that building and its owner, your typical American asshole who thought he could bribe his way into building a high-rise condo tower in a town with a four-story height limit. But they claim to have stopped him with some sort of legal maneuver, and he's actually taking the top floors down now. Anyways those other little buildings on the hillside are hotel rooms, and they looked really cool on the Web."

"Whatever," said Marcia. "I'm going to get my board." She dashed off down the beach, the eyes of several young Mexican surf-dudes following her. Kept company by half a dozen panting mongrel dogs, they lolled on the sand in the shade of the *X Dames* pavilion, watching the waves, drinking beer, and checking out the girls.

"Those waves are pretty fockin' serious, as they say down in Oz," Lucy said. The bigger outside waves looked about twice the height of the surfers dropping into them. Walls of white water rolled in, one after another, as the surfers paddled, caught waves, rode them or crashed, all the while shouting at each other. The big waves had them cranked up. "Looks like really intense conditions for a contest to me. Hope Bobby has enough sense to keep the ringers out of the water."

"How about you, Luce?" said Teresa. "Would you paddle out there?"

"Paddle out, yes," Lucy said. "It'll be great for shooting up close. My camera's waterproof. And I can paddle pretty well from swimming and working out. But I couldn't ride those waves. I've only surfed like five times and I just don't know enough."

"Excuse me, ladies," a man interrupted them. They turned. He was forty or so, a handsome tall Mexican in carefully pressed khaki shorts, black leather sandals, and a loose-fitting, well-made sport shirt and sunglasses. "Are you—"

"Teresa MacDonald." She held out a hand. "And Lucy Ripken. You must be—"

"Ruben Dario. From the show. And a local here as well. So nice to meet you. I hope you traveled well. Come join us, please." He gestured at one of the larger tables at the front edge of El Costeño, which faced out to the surf. There were three women seated there, comfortably slouched in tiny bikinis. One was Asian, the other two were Mexican, and they were uniformly brown, lithe, long-haired, and beautiful in the modern way, physically confident, fierce, fearless, and yet utterly feminine. Powerbabes, soon to rule the world. As she and Terry followed Dario to the table,

Lucy thought, any TV show that's got this trio, plus Marcia, Henrietta, and Sandra, all of them out there in those waves, is going to rock!

"So where's the lovely Henrietta?" said Moki Sue Kalahana'I, the twenty-six-year-old "surf dominatrix," after they did the meet and greet, sat down, and ordered beers. The other two at the table were Martina Casals, a twenty-year-old Mexican girl famous for a videotaped tube ride she'd grabbed at Puerto Escondido, the renowned Mexican Pipeline, down the coast in Oaxaca. Martina had entirely disappeared inside this ten-foot tube for five seconds and then came flying out still on her feet, with a huge smile on her face and the top half of her bathing suit blown off and away by the wind and spray inside the tube. Needless to say, that topless tube ride lived on in the land of endless loops on TV and the Internet, and Martina had become one of the five or six most famous female surfers in the world as a result. And finally there was Erica Nuñez, over thirty, but four times in a row the Mexican women's surfing champion. She had pretty much the same body as the other two, five and a half foot tall smoothly muscled girls in impossibly great shape. Neither she nor Martina spoke English very well, so Dario, the only bilingualist among them, carried the conversation.

"I have no idea," said Teresa. "I thought she came down with Bobby and all the TV people."

"Yes, I saw her this morning at the house Bobby's rented," Dario said. "Don't worry, Señorita Moki, she's on it. She wants that money as much as you do." He smiled.

"And have you writer ladies concocted some interesting—narratives—for our girls to pursue?"

"We sure have," Terry said. "We wrote the whole damn show on the plane coming down here today."

"This is good," he said, then turned and did some explaining in Spanish. The two Mexican girls laughed.

"What?" said Lucy, hating her own lack of Spanish. "What's so funny?"

"Oh, I was just telling them about how much Moki Sue wants to beat Sandra's butt and everybody else too, but especially Henrietta's. And they think it is funny that all these gringas are so intent on beating each other that they don't realize that the Mexican girls are the best surfers here at their home beach."

"Hm," said Teresa. "Sounds like a challenge—and a plotline."

"Hey, gang," Marcia said, breathlessly arriving at the table. "The hotel's cool." She wore a dinky bikini bottom and a short-sleeved rash-guard top in neo-psychedelic colors, and carried under one arm a short, skinny little board, maybe five and a half feet long. Her sickly pallor had gone away as if by magic in the Mexican sun, and she looked like a red-hot surfer girl, ready to rule some waves.

Lucy did a quick intro, then Marcia said, "So why aren't all you big-time wave-bombing surf-chicks out there now? Too hairy for you? Those waves look awesome!"

"Because they were better this morning at high tide, Chiquita," said Moki Sue. "And we're saving it because we are competing tomorrow and we all surfed for three hours today." She turned to Teresa. "So why is this girl in the contest? A little T&A bimbo to fill in the background? Or are you a hot surfer, too, little girl?" she sneered.

"See you in the waves, *puta* bitch," Marcia said as she turned and headed towards the water.

"Ouch! Girl's got a short temper," Moki Sue said with a grin. "Can't take a joke."

"It wasn't funny," said Lucy. "And she's a good surfer so don't take her too lightly."

Moki Sue gave Lucy an appraising look. "So what are you going to write about that? How I insulted one of my competitors and—"

"Personal vendettas and hurt feelings are fodder for the plot," said Terry, "so keep it up." She turned to Lucy. "Seems like we already have our villain in place."

"Hey," Moki Sue said. "Don't typecast me. I'm not your Dragon Lady bad girl. I just want to win, like everybody else. The mind game's part of the gameplan."

Terry glared at her. "Hey, that wasn't about racial shit, that was—"

"Excuse me, ladies," said Dario. "I wanted to ask our writers here—" Lucy and Teresa gave him their attention. "I'm already organizing the next segment after the surf contest. Did Bobby mention our plans? Will you be able to travel to South America from here to work on the snowboarding competition next week? My partner Sophie has been down there scouting locations, and it looks like she has lined up a great mountain with a fully equipped lodge, reliable lifts, and excellent powder snow, in the Chilean

Andes. The feeling is if we can alternate winter and summer sports it will create a great dynamic for the series, I think to give it that global feeling."

"Chile? Next week? Jesus, I don't know. I've got a book to finish. Luce, what do you think?"

"Hey, look at that," Lucy said, quickly whipping a small pair of high-powered binoculars out of her bag. "Is that Marcia?" She focused. "Yes. She's caught a monster wave." They all watched as the girl stood up on her board at the top of a huge wave, then dropped in. When she hit bottom it was evident the wave's face was nearly three times her height, at least fifteen feet high. She hit the bottom on her little short board, carved a big, smooth turn, and climbed up the face of the wave at high speed. At the top she whipped a slashing cutback, and her board broke loose of the water, freefalling down the face. Her feet hardly touched the board until it hit water near the wave's bottom, when she somehow landed perfectly balanced and executed another big turn, this one ending with a lunging kickout over the top as a collapsing section closed the wave out.

They were quiet for a few seconds, taking it in. Then Moki Sue said, "Holy shit! That girl can surf!"

"*Magnífico*," said Dario. "And what a mighty wave!"

Martina said, "Thees ees I theenk the wave of the day so far. It is like Puerto Es only not so breaking hard as there."

"Judy told me the swell's going to peak tomorrow," said Teresa. "So it could be even bigger for the contest."

"Hey, I'm from Hawaii," said Moki Sue. "I eat waves like these for lunch."

They all looked at her. "Chow down, baby," said Lucy.

Next morning Lucy awoke from her usual restless sleep just before sunrise to the rhythmic rising and falling roar of big waves breaking in a steady, swell-driven surge. She knew from the sound that it would be large out there, possibly larger even than the day before. Like every ocean-lover Lucy got an elemental charge from the sight and sound of big surf, but before she would permit herself the thrill of getting out of bed to throw open her curtains for a look at the wave-crazed bay, she forced herself to lie still and recall as distinctly as she could, through the unpleasantness of a minor tequila hangover, the events of last night. For purposes of *X Dames* plotting, and also to soothe her soul. It had been a long, strange evening.

After settling into their suite, the three women had chilled out for a short break, then dressed for dinner *tres casual, tres chic*, short summer dresses and sandals all, and headed out. It took about half an hour to walk from their hotel to La Casa de la Luna Grande, or the House of the Big Fat Moon, as they translated it: first a stroll a few hundred yards down a dirt road that paralleled the curve of Sayulita's rocky south end beach, then a jog to the right to the town square, where hippie vagabonds sold jeweled tchotchkes, and Mexican kids played soccer between the palm trees while their parents sold tacos, DVDs, toilet brushes, plastic action heroes, and other useful stuff from ramshackle little stands around the plaza's edges. Clusters of half-drunk, sun-roasted north-end gringos noisily roamed in search of the perfect fish taco, while their downscale surfer and hippie brethren loitered on low walls and benches in the plaza, guzzling Pacifico beer from fat liter bottles or margaritas from plastic cups. Music blared out of radios, bars, cars, and restaurants. Everybody looked slightly buzzed and vacantly pleased with themselves. What could be better than a beach vacation in a foreign town where you could stumble down the street somewhat wasted, with little chance of getting insulted, robbed, arrested, run over, or blown to pieces?

From this festive arena the three women crossed the bridge and made their way to the beach road. After passing a large soccer pitch and a couple of shabby old two-story hotels, derelict construction sites, and the fenced and gated grounds of the town school, they entered the posh precincts of the north end, where the houses on the beach to the left, and on the hills rising up to the right, took on a more grandiose, even pompous, bearing, and enormous, dusty SUVs rumbled past, bearing gringos downtown. This was monied territory, on both sides of the road. One of the last houses on the beach was La Casa de la Luna Grande. Bobby Schamberg had rented it for two weeks for six grand. Staying with him in the main house were Judy and Henrietta, with Mary Miles and her pair of executive producer boys ensconced in the guesthouse by the pool. Excepting the Mexican surfer girls and Sandra Darwin, who lived in town, everybody else involved with the show had holed up at the Villa Roma. Ruben Dario, who summered in a beachfront manse in Santa Barbara, had his own hacienda, said to be the biggest house in town, on the hill overlooking the north end and the bay.

They made their entrance. The house included a huge veranda overlooking the north end beach, where heavy shorebreak surf pounded on the rocks scarcely fifty feet from where the gang sat down to dinner after killing two bottles of tequila in half a cocktail hour. While the waves rattled the crockery, they ate gourmet mex surrounded by waiters, fast-moving cameramen, lighting and sound guys, makeup artists, and assorted stylists, all directed by Mary Miles's assistant director, a Mexican-American guy called Hector Valdez. Mary was nowhere to be seen, having retired early to her guesthouse with her pair of boy EPs in tow and "a horny gleam in her eye," as Bobby smirkingly put it. Turned out Mary was a rapacious boy-chaser but that was definitely not part of the *X Dames* narrative. The crew busily shot video-tape from every possible direction, planning to plug footage from this intro dinner into *X Dames* Episode One.

Along with the surfer girls Lucy had already met, and Bobby and his posse, there were a couple of local notables on hand: Ruben Dario, of course, for he was a major player in this *X Dames* game. Also present was Wally Townsend, Dario's American partner in the realty end of his business interests. Between them they had sold sixteen Sayulita houses over the past winter, and currently had eleven more in escrow. Although they weren't demonstrably affec-tionate, judging by what Lucy saw in the course of the well-documented evening, Ruben Dario and the Amazon surf-queen Sandra Darwin possibly had a thing going on.

The other guest was a man called *El Pantero*, the panther, a dark-skinned, muscular, and gorgeous mestizo from Puerto Escondido, famed for surfing Puerto's heavy, scary tubes with the cunning grace of a large, predatory cat. Hence the name. With his luminous black eyes and his ripped, cat-like body, topped by a ridiculously sexy shock of dyed blond hair, the panther was hotter than hot, and he knew it.

Through the evening, several semi-planned spats erupted among the surf-chicks—these babes were quickly learning how to make reality more real for the cameras, and so, urged on by Terry and Hector both, Moki Sue merrily belittled the surfing skills of her competitors, especially Marcia and Henrietta, who retaliated in kind.

Trapped between Dario and Townsend, Lucy missed out on the girly melodrama and instead made useful small talk with the Realtors. Dario, who was half-Mexican and half-Californian and possessed dual citizenship, seemingly had married into one of Sayulita's wealthy families years back. He was rich, arrogant, and all-knowing, while Townsend, American salesman type to the rotten core, kissed Dario's ass. From the two of them Lucy learned how the *Ejido* system worked. Before the recently enacted law allowing gringos to buy houses via bank trusts had passed, the only way for gringos to own property in Mexico was with a Mexican partner, called a *prestanombre*, whose name would go on the deed along with the gringo name. These paper partnerships of convenience, formed under edicts proclaimed by each municipal council, or *Ejido*, were accompanied by powers of attorney which prevented the Mexican *prestanombres* from doing anything with the houses, such as buying, selling, renting, occupying or otherwise using them to their own advantage; and if properly written, the powers of attorney allowed the American partners to do what they wanted without the Mexican partner's permission. Dario served as *prestanombre* for over fifty houses in Sayulita, he claimed.

With roots in both Sayulita and Southern California, Dario had been a serious surfer a few years back. Since he was also a big shot around town, he had been anointed an *X Dames* surfing contest judge. The surf champion *El Pantero* was the second judge, and Judy Leggett, former American women's champion, served as the third.

Judy maintained a low profile through the evening, and Lucy wondered what it was—other than Judy's weird replay of the knife-to-the-nostril scene from Chinatown— that had triggered her suspicions in the first place. Here in Sayulita, off her own turf, Judy seemed a non-player. Terry said she thought the woman was stoned on codeine or opiates, easy to come by from a Mexican pharmacy, but who knew?

In any case, the show's mix seemingly was rich with potential strife and conflict. Good material.

As was her habit at large, loud dinners, when not making small talk Lucy watched. And so she watched—Marcia. After she'd downed several shots of tequila and at least five beers, Marcia ended up coming on hot, cheap, and heavy to Ruben Dario. Lucy knew why: he'd been sneaking smoldering Latin lover-man glances at Marcia every chance he got. And she fell for it, for at heart, Lucy was certain, Marcia remained an innocent in spite of her Goth hair, surf-Goth style, and her possibly evil drug habits. Dario was handsome, wealthy, once a renowned surfer, now a man of the world. All in all, a major temptation for a girl like Marcia.

The two other serious surfer girls, from San Diego, were due in at midnight. Bobby had trolled the beaches of Sayulita that very day, *X Dames* checkbook in hand, and found four other hot babes and signed them up to fill in the competitive ranks. However, the two Canadian sisters, the Japanese exchange student, and the Colombian hippie girl were not actually surfing or even paddling out, due to the unusually large waves. Instead they would stand on the beach in their itsy-bitsys—they all had great bods, of course, and Bobby would provide the bikini if anyone didn't have the right one—with surfboards at hand, gazing out wistfully and shaking their heads. Surf's too much for us. We'll have to leave it to the pros. This would enhance the already awesome reps of those dames brave enough to paddle out in this once-in-a-decade monster swell. It was shaping up to be a wild, wild scene. Made for TV.

And then as the night wound down, somewhere in the mists of tequila-land *El Pantero* had made a move on her, Lucy Ripken. After staring at her intermittently with his bad kitty black eyes at the table, and flashing his lovely white-fanged smile her way to further signal his interest, he caught her in an unguarded moment as she emerged from a 600-square-foot bathroom designed to mimic a jungle grotto, and there among the lilies and orchids and rustling green leaves he almost convinced her that an amorous tumble in her posh, king-sized hotel bed would be worth the next day's regrets; but no, at the last possible instant, before her inhibitions simply melted away in the heated urgency of the panther's desire, she slipped away, back to the table, strewn with tequila bottles, and sat her ass down to draw a deep breath and consider her options; and then a skewed glance across that same table at Teresa, stone cold sober, watching her with concerned eyes, had shut down her libido. And so instead of humping the panther, soon thereafter she slipped out the door with Teresa, and the two of them trudged home side by side, holding hands on a long, pleasantly sobering mile's walk down the sands of Sayulita's beach, from the north end to the south, mulling their own less-endangered fates in the shadow of the fate of young Marcia, wasted on tequila and beer. They had left her to fend for herself. Back at the Villa Roma they'd sat up for half an hour taking notes on the evening's doings, plotting, plotting—and then crashed in their separate bedrooms. Marcia hadn't shown up to claim the third bedroom by the time they went to sleep.

And now another day. Lucy got up and pulled the curtains and the sliding glass doors open, then jumped back into bed, drew the sheet up over her naked self, and gazed out, listening to the loud but strangely soothing roar of the sea. Across the dirt road, through the picture-framing trunks of coconut palms, in the misty morning light, on a glass-smooth surface the big waves broke, one after another, six to ten foot faces, clean lines in the sunrise light, surfing perfection on an epic day at Sayulita Beach. At this sleepy hour she could see just three early-bird wave hounds out, scoring perfect right-breaking waves one after another. She watched a guy drop into an eight-footer, only to blow his bottom turn, lulled by a slow-peeling wave-lip that suddenly collapsed, sending him into a crash and burn under several tons of furious white water.

Big surf, half a dozen hot wave-riding girls, and after last night, enough plot potential to drive the *X Dames* for a season, if need be. Like Mary had said, just put them all in a room, or in this case an ocean, and let them be themselves.

She put on a plush terrycloth robe she found hanging on the bathroom door, then banged on the door to the next bedroom. "Yo, Ter, time to shake it. Showtime, hon." She heard a murmur, and went in. Zonked out flat on her back in the middle of her kingsizer, Terry was covered by her sheet from head to toe, like a corpse. "Hey, get your booty moving, girl," Lucy said. "The surf is way up and we have a TV show to invent."

"Yeah, yeah," Terry said, pulling the sheet down and sitting up in bed in her sleeping T-shirt. "You know me, Luce. Morning's not my best time."

"Did our Miss Marcia make it home?" Lucy asked, nodding at the door to the next bedroom.

Teresa shrugged. "I don't know. I took half an Ambien to make sure I slept."

"Do you have any to spare? I hear that stuff works and doesn't mess you up. A good night's sleep would be a godsend. Jesus, I hope Marcia didn't chase that Dario home," Lucy said. "He was throwing bedroom eyes at her all night, right in front of his girlfriend—or I guess the appropriate word would be mistress."

"I noticed. So did she. Sandra, I mean."

"So did everybody. It'll be on prime time. Marcia's none too subtle. Which makes her perfect for reality TV, doesn't it?"

"Yep. Hey, where's coffee? I need coffee. The Ambien may not fuck you up but it definitely clogs your head."

"Everybody's coming here for breakfast on the veranda in . . ." Lucy looked at her watch. "Twenty minutes. Then it's down to the beach to get the first heat started. They're thinking about getting the whole contest done today, while the waves are smoking." Lucy felt totally wired. This was reality TV. With big waves and red-hot girls to ride them, it was sure to be really good fun.

5

Big Trouble in the Big Waves

Lucy put her black one-piece on under pink shorts and a black T-shirt, stepped into her flip-flops, and methodically packed a bag with her waterproof digital camera, towel, SPF 30 waterproof sunscreen, shades, collapsible sun hat, three lipsticks, hairbrush, Spanish phrasebook, pack of sugarless gum, and five hundred pesos. About fifty bucks. She knocked on Teresa's door, went in, found her dressed and ready to roll, then crossed to the next door. She knocked. No answer. Knocked again, a little harder.

"Momentito, por favor." A man's muffled voice. They looked at each other.

"The plot thickens," Terry said.

"Want to guess who?" Lucy said.

"Ten bucks says its Dario."

"My bet's on Bobby."

"No way. He's already babed-up. Besides, why would he speak Spanish?"

"He thinks I'm a maid."

Lucy banged harder on the door, then waited. It opened after a moment. Wrapped in a towel, bleached hair sticking straight up, a shit-eating grin on his face, there stood *El Pantero*. "Fuck," Lucy said, plunged into a sudden whirl of a state: dismay, jealousy, insecurity, anger. Take your choice. "What the hell are you doing here?" she said.

He shrugged, and grinned. "Miss Marcia—she—ah—invites me. So I come." Marcia emerged from her bathroom, naked, toweling her long black hair dry. She was slender, muscular, small-breasted; perfect, and eleven years younger than Lucy. And Lucy could not help but notice that her pubic hair had been—styled? Trimmed and groomed? What was the correct description? The Brazilian was a complete shave; Lucy knew that much. But this was more of a—landing strip!

"Hi Lucy," she said, completely guileless. "What's up?"

Lucy gazed at her, attempting inscrutability. "Are you ready to compete today, or are you so fucked-up that—"

"Stop it, Luce," Terry said evenly, from across the room. "Don't go there."

"You're right," Lucy said, tone gone flat. She looked at her watch, then at Marcia, who met her stare head-on.

"I'm fine, Lucy. Yes I got drunk last night and I slept with this guy and we fucked like two or three times but I insisted on all the necessary precautions and now I feel just fine. I'm ready to rock."

"Breakfast's on the terrace across the street in seven minutes," Lucy said. Maybe it would be harder going than she'd expected, befriending Marcia Hobgood. "Be there." She closed the door, and looked at Teresa. "I guess we both lost that bet, eh?"

"Aren't you glad *you* didn't bring that dickhead back here last night?"

"You might say that. Obviously the guy's a horndog, wanted to fuck whoever."

"Well what did you think, he was in love with you?"

"Please shut up now, Ter," Lucy said, but she was smiling. "So I'm stupid sometimes."

"You weren't stupid, Luce. You were *almost* stupid."

By seven-thirty they had assembled on the Villa Roma's immaculately groomed grass terrace overlooking the rocky south end of Sayulita Beach. They sat in white wrought iron chairs around a long white oval-shaped wrought iron table sculpted with fleur-de-lis and such. The Villa Roma fancied itself fancy. Lucy found herself seated next to Sandra Darwin at one end of the table, closest to the steps leading down to the beach. Sandra was distracted, tense, intent, eyes mostly on the waves awaiting her. Lucy knew she wanted this one bad. All the surfer girls were present, including the two from San Diego who'd arrived late—Bev and Charlene, a pair of hard-charging, thirtyish blondes, perennial surf-contest also-rans but good enough to fill the *X Dames* ranks, and on a good day capable of an upset win. They both featured the sculpted, angular faces and lanky musculature Lucy had come to associate with serious women surfers. Also on hand were the four ringers Bobby had gathered up on the beach the day before. Six more women to go with the Hot Surf Six, and all possessed of a strong, sexy vibe. Hector and the other camera guys roamed the periphery, documenting every moment of drama at table, as four waiters in black pants, white shirts, and black bow ties delivered platters of fruit salad, eggs, beans, toast, bacon, chiles rellenos, and tortillas along with pitchers of coffee, milk, fresh orange juice, and bottles of champagne. Among the surfer girls only Marcia, tucked in between Moki Sue and *El Pantero* near the other end of the table, hit the bottle. Lucy counted three brimming re-fills. In the background, across two hundred yards of churning ocean, the waves cracked and roared, a dozen local surf-kids slicing and dicing them in a hurry to get it while they could, before the *X Dames* Sayulita Surf-babe Throwdown took over.

They ate and chattered, while the crew filmed on. The drama had turned quiet: a bit of sexual undertow, and the girls anxiously looking out to sea. No time for bullshit-ting now, with the tension building. For all the Hollywood hype and the sexy babe business and the sideshow insults, there was a surfing contest about to start, and the waves out there loomed big and fast and unforgiving. These girls were up against the real thing.

Eventually, Bobby tapped a spoon on a glass a few times, then stood and cleared his throat. He took off his shades and smiled his sexiest Hollywood producer smile. "Well here we are, gang. And this is it: Showtime. Never in my wildest dreams about how this show would work did I imagine that we would have a set-up like this for the first episode. Like Henrietta told me last night, 'The surf out there is fucking ferocious, man.' And that it is," he said, looking towards the waves. "So I'm only going to waste one more minute of your time before we get on with it, because I wanted to say thanks to my partner Judy Leggett for steering us to Sayulita after we decided to start with a surfing contest. What a great little town it's turned out to be. And thanks to Teresa MacDonald and Lucy Ripken for agreeing to come down here on short notice to help organize the story. And to Ruben Dario and Sandra Darwin for setting things up. Thanks to all you crew dudes, and Mary, our fine director. And most of all thanks to the girls," he raised a glass of champagne, "for sticking your butts on the line by signing up to paddle out in that maelstrom to compete. I for one am not going to even get my toes into that crazy ocean today. You is one brave bunch of dames. So here's a toast to the *X Dames*." Bravos and applause. He went on. "So I know you're all wondering how it's going to work, right? Well, we decided in the interests of showbiz to keep it simple. Also the waves being so large, we thought you ladies might get worn out if things went on too long. So this is it: two thirty-minute heats, six surfers in each— well, four, since I suspect our last four entrants may end up on the beach, where I found them and where they belong, watching. We count the best six rides, you score points from one to ten, ten being tops. Each judge scores each ride, then we average out the three scores. Two advance from each heat, leaving four in the final. The final's one hour, same deal only you'll get scored on ten rides. Judy's wave-tracker guy says this is the last day of the swell and its probably going to start fading this afternoon so we're planning to do the whole shoot today, probably try to squeeze the final in before lunch too if we can. Time is money in showbiz, and today the surf's on the clock too." He looked at his watch. "It's eight-forty-five. First heat's at ten. Everybody should be down at the pavilion by nine-thirty. That's it. Do your best, girls." He sat down. Judy whispered something to him. "Oh," he stood again and went on. "I almost forgot. You know this already but just in case it slipped your mind, the prize for winning today is twenty-five thousand U.S. dollars and an invite to the next round of *X Dames* with its hundred grand first prize payoff. I think you all know the drill. We'll take one winner from each of six or eight sports, put them in a ring with a bunch of starving lions, and whoever survives gets the hundred grand. Hehe, just kidding. No, the finals are still in the works. We're honestly thinking about hiring trainers from Thailand and teaching our individual winners to kick-box, so that we can have a real fight to the finish. But the main thing is today we got some world-class waves, and you girls have a chance to strut your stuff and launch episode one with some sexy surfing. And so—may the best dame win. Everybody else, well, you got a paid vacation in Mexico." The waiters began clearing the table and the cast and crew of the *X Dames* collected their paraphernalia and surfboards and headed down the road to the beach. Showtime.

"Remember, Lucy, timing is everything when you're paddling out," said Marcia. "Get as close as you can to the impact zone, where the waves are breaking, while there's a set on. Then when the set is over paddle your ass off and hope you make it outside before the next set comes." She'd been solicitous ever since they got up from the breakfast table and grabbed their gear, having figured out in her thick young head that she'd hurt Lucy's feelings. Of course, Marcia was slightly drunk from at least four glasses of champagne at breakfast; plus Lucy had seen Teresa reading Marcia the riot act as they walked down the road together, so this act of contrition was a bit contrived. Whatever. It wasn't like Lucy really had a right to be pissed, and she knew it. She had eluded the panther last night, and so he'd continued the hunt, and found other prey.

Lucy stood between Marcia and Sandra, each carrying shortboards, waiting for the moment. Lucy had Marcia's Mayan snake-patterned longboard under one arm and her camera with an extra-long strap double-looped around her neck and clutched in her free hand. Stretchy rubber leashes with Velcro end-straps connected the boards to the women's ankles, so that if they took a wipeout the boards wouldn't get carried on the waves all the way to the beach. They wore rash-guard shirts, all but Lucy's numbered so the judges would know who was who. An air horn had blown at 9:30 to signal to all the surfers in the water to head shorewards. Now it was 9:50 and the last seventeen-year-old Mexican surf-punk had just come ashore, pissed that his hometown wave had been jacked for the contest during the best swell he'd ever seen in Sayulita. He sneered, going past. The first heat girls ignored him. Marcia and Sandra, flanking Lucy, stood at water's edge in the cove; Martina and Bev had decided to hit the water forty yards up the beach. All five of them looked out to sea, making their calculations.

Standing between the buff young surfer girls, Lucy wondered what she felt she had to prove—why she'd decided she had to go out there and shoot stills from the water. They had a video camcorder guy up on the judges' stand with enough digital telephoto power to see the whites of their eyes, two hundred yards offshore; Mary and Bobby could easily grab stills from his tape. They had another camera guy with full telephoto power patrolling the beach, and a third in a waverunner cruising outside the break.

And yet she'd volunteered to get out there in the swim to shoot. Macho Lucy in action, planting herself in the middle of things because she felt compelled to compete with these girls yet didn't know how to surf well enough. She'd only surfed half a dozen times, and these were far bigger than any waves she'd ever paddled into. Pushing her limits, taking that risk, that's what it was all about. She did want to get good pictures, but ultimately the camera was just an excuse.

And she knew her own subtext; her backstory, as they called it in Hollywood. This was also about her anger at Marcia for sleeping with the panther, even though Lucy had turned him down earlier in the evening. She hated pushing thirty-five. She hated even thinking about feeling old, and she hated herself for letting it get to her. But it did.

Yet on the other hand she knew that it would help with plot-writing if she could see how the women interacted out there, how it played out in the waves, with their reputations, twenty-five grand, and God knew what else on the line. It would be great, intense fun to stick herself in the lineup and get some close-ups.

She glanced back. A sunny, windless, eighty-degree late spring morning in Sayulita. Several hundred people sat on lounge chairs beneath umbrellas, or stood in the sand near the judges' stand, or roamed the beach, all pleased that simply by being on vacation this particular week they'd stumbled into a television surf-circus featuring a dozen bodacious babes and a real-life Hollyweird vibe. Up on the judges' stand Lucy could see Judy, *El Pantero*, and Ruben Dario, clipboards in hand and binoculars at the ready, with a couple of assistants close by—and a cameraman on a stepladder above them all, his camcorder roving from the contestants, to the crowds, to the waves cracking and roaring two hundred yards offshore. The four other competing girls, already suited up in their numbered rash-guard shirts, loitered by the judge stand waiting for the second heat. As expected the four ringers hadn't even bothered to put on rash-guards. Per instructions from Mary Miles, they were hanging around the pavilion in thong-style bikinis, exposing major butt and boob and reveling in their fabulous fifteen minutes while being interviewed by a guy from Mexican TV news while Hector taped them. In their divers charming accents each explained why she couldn't possibly go out in such crazy, dangerous surf. Lucy and Teresa had fed them their lines after breakfast.

Lucy could be up there now with Teresa, monitoring the action, self-importantly playing the writer on location, but instead she had talked herself right into the thick of it. She was about to paddle a longboard out into the biggest waves she'd ever seen. Teresa, at the edge of the pavilion, gave her the thumbs up, and then the airhorn sounded again.

"This is it, girls," said Sandra. "Good luck out there," she said to Marcia. "And keep your longboard butt out of my way, Lucy," she added, smiling as she said it.

"Chaaaarge," screamed Marcia, dashing for the water and leaping onto her board to start her frantic paddle to the outside, where the breaking waves awaited them. Sandra was right behind her. Up the beach, Bev and Martina dashed and leaped onto their boards. The race was on to see who would get out and grab the first wave of the contest.

Lucy took a slightly more cautious approach, moving a little farther into the water, then waiting for a wall of white water to rush around her legs. She slung her camera onto her back, laid down on the board, and began a fast, steady paddle out, using the receding white water, so powerful it almost qualified as a riptide, to push her along.

Fifteen of the longest minutes of her life later, Lucy, wasted to the point of near-unconsciousness, lunged over the top of an eight-foot wave and thanked Jesus, Buddha, and Lord Krishna, too, that she made it over that one, and she thanked her divers deities as well for the momentarily calm sea before her: that was the last wave of the set. She had made it! Only shoving under, over, or through six major walls of white water, and at least twenty minor ones, had taken every last ounce of her strength, and now she verged on a physical meltdown. She paddle-dragged herself a dozen yards farther out, and a moment later was joined by Sandra.

"Did you shoot my first wave?" Sandra said. "It was awesome."

"Are you crazy? I barely survived getting out here," Lucy panted.

"Like Marcia said, it's all timing, Lucy. Hey, chickie, I think I just scored a ten," she called out to Martina, "and I didn't even have to take my top off." Martina ignored her, not getting the insult in English. "Uh oh, Luce," said Sandra, "here comes another set. And it looks like a big one." She shook her head. "Damn," she said. "My energy's really low this morning. I must have had one too many shots of Sauza last night." She shook her head again as she paddled towards the rising horizon, with Lucy, Martina, and now Marcia and Bev behind them, racing to get in position to grab one of the next waves.

Lucy felt wiped out. Usually a minute's rest after a burn would bring her back, but she was feeling slower, less responsive, as she paddled the longboard, camera on the deck in front of her. Beyond the waves, she could hear the insect buzz of the waverunner, a higher tone above the roaring surf. She angled to her left, towards the waves' shoulders, while the competitors paddled to the right, to get in better position to catch one in the steeper section.

As the first set wave moved over the rocky reef on the bottom it pitched up to about ten feet high, and steepened radically. Marcia, closest to the break, whipped her board around and with a single stroke caught it, stood, and dropped in. Lucy, forty yards down the line, started shooting. Marcia hit the bottom of the wave at full speed and then using that speed threw a fast turn and flew up the face at a sharp angle towards the lip, and then when she hit the lip instead of carving back she went airborne, grabbed a rail, and somehow, impossibly, she whipped her board around and completed an aerial 360 and landed on her feet on the board on the face of the wave. She dropped to the bottom and as the wave began to close out ahead of her raced back to the top and flew over and out.

Lucy had captured maybe fifteen images in ten endless seconds, and so she knew that regardless of what had been taped from the beach, she had still photographs of what had to be one of the most amazing surfing maneuvers she had ever seen pulled off by anyone, male or female. Lucy had watched plenty of footage and no one did 360 aerials on waves that large. No one except the half-drunk speed-abusing star-fucking wannabe artist, Marcia Hobgood. What she had just done was nothing short of miraculous, athletically speaking.

Then the next wave came and Lucy, busily shooting, barely cleared the lip as she paddled over. Bev caught it, dropped into a bottom turn, raced down the line, and then slashed a huge cutback close enough to shower Lucy with a rainbow spray. And then the next, and biggest, wave rose up, and Sandra Darwin, in perfect position, paddled twice and caught it. As she slipped down the face, her hands slid out from under her as she tried to push up off the board onto her feet and she headed straight down at full speed into a pearl dive, face planted on the board deck. The wave crashed and she disappeared under it. Lucy had it all on camera, shot from the lip down the line. The board bobbed up, twenty yards closer to shore. Sandra popped up a few seconds later. She was maybe a hundred feet away by then, and so Lucy couldn't be sure if Sandra looked over at her and meekly called out the word "help," or if she, Lucy, only imagined it. Then Sandra slowly flopped over, and went face down. "Help! We need help here," Lucy cried out. "Sandra's down," she yelled, but there was no one close enough to hear. Martina blasted by on the next wave, the white water behind her slamming Sandra and her board, sending her under again. Clinging to her longboard, Lucy barely cleared the wave. Behind it there was another, larger one; charging in front of that next wave, the waverunner, with two guys on it—pilot and cameraman—raced furiously towards Sandra, intent on a rescue. Lucy watched, firing away even as she felt herself sliding up the face of the wave, afloat on her longboard and trying to paddle as she realized that she was not going to get over the top—and that she was losing consciousness. She watched helplessly as the wave that was about to throw her over the falls and down to the bottom of the sea lifted the waverunner with two men and a large video camera up on its breaking crest and then tumbled down directly upon the floating body and board of Sandra Darwin, and then Lucy too was gone into darkness.

6

Let's Go to the Video

Upon awakening alive and comfortable in a cushy bed, Lucy murmured, "Ouch. My head hurts." Then she heard the cries of seagulls above the soft call of the surf. She opened her eyes. She lay atop the covers on her hotel room bed, her hotel bathrobe draped over her body. Terry sat on one side, Marcia on the other, both looking concerned. Warm sunset light angled in the open doors, and a faint breeze swayed the white curtains. "Jesus, what happened? What time is it? How did I get here?"

"It's almost five o'clock," Terry said. "You've been out for like six or seven hours."

"Out? What do you mean, out? I was in the water, and—Oh my God, what happened? What happened to Sandra?"

Terry and Marcia exchanged glances. "I got to you, Lucy," said Marcia. "But not her. I was paddling back out and both you and Sandra had wiped out. It was insane out there. I was closer to you and you were going under after that wave threw you over the falls so I came after you. I think Sandra must have gotten hit by her board because she was face-down in the water like she was unconscious. Those poor fools on the waverunner tried to get to her, and instead, they got snatched up by that giant wave and crashed right down on top of her."

"People think she may have already drowned," said Terry. "But it looked like the collision fractured her skull as well. It was a total disaster. The waverunner guys barely made it to the beach alive, and they lost a ten-thousand-dollar camera and the waverunner. They got them both back when the waves finally backed down and the tide went out this afternoon but both are completely ruined, and the camera guy broke his arm."

"Jesus Christ," Lucy whispered. "God, thanks for saving my ass, Marcia. I don't know what happened out there, but—"

"You shouldn't have been out in that surf, Luce," Terry said. "It was too big."

"But what about the contest? What happened to the contest?"

"That crazy fuck Bobby insisted that they keep going," Terry said. "First Marcia hauled you onto your board and somehow she got the two of you in by riding this giant wall of white water sideways on the longboard, then we dragged you up on the beach, and after a few seconds of mouth-to-mouth you woke up, tossed about a quart of saltwater, took a deep breath, and looked at me. God, I was so happy to see you open your eyes I cried. Jesus, Lucy, that was way too close."

"Then you looked at me," said Marcia. "And said 'what the hell happened?' and passed back out. But you were breathing normally so we laid you down in the shade and Terry sat with you to make sure you were OK. Then Martina brought Sandra in like five minutes later, and Bobby and Dario scooped her up and wrapped her in a towel and Townsend volunteered to take her away to the hospital in Puerto Vallarta but a couple of us saw her, and her head looked really bad. Like smashed in. I swear to God to me it looked like she was already dead, Lucy. I don't know, but . . ." her voice quavered. Then she took a deep breath and went on. "Dario's her fucking boyfriend, and he saw her too, and he didn't even want to go to the hospital." She hesitated. "But he's a heartless bastard and I think your friend Bobby's a Hollywood psycho, so after we got both of you onto the beach, I couldn't believe it, Bobby was like, on with the show. We didn't know what to say or do at that point; to tell the truth I was kind of in shock, but anyways me and Martina paddled back out like trained dogs and got some more waves. Since Bev wasn't quite at our level, at least in those big waves, me and Martina made the finals.

"Then Henrietta and Moki Sue took the second heat over Charlene and Erica, no problem, no accidents, no weird shit. Then we all sat on the beach for half an hour not saying a word."

Teresa cut in: "Bobby and Judy and the *X Dames* people were walking around all solemn, playing up how the drama of the contest had been heightened by the 'accident' and shit, I mean they were just feeding off the tragedy like jack-als, Lucy, it was disgusting. And I know that's exactly what he wants us to do with whatever the fuck else we write, too. I tell you I'm ready to walk."

Marcia said, "Anyways me and the other girls were all too freaked out to do anything except what they told us. I swear to God we were numb and dumb—so then the four of us went back into the waves for the final."

"And Marcia simply kicked ass," Terry said. "She won hands down."

"You won? That's great!"

"Fuck it. It isn't great at all. Not with what happened to Sandra."

"But still, as they say, the show must go on."

"I guess. Yeah. Right," said Marcia. "The show. Fuck the show."

"Well, think of the twenty-five grand, and art school, and . . . "

"It's blood money, Lucy."

"Come on, Marcia, don't say that. You didn't do anything. . . ."

"Other than save Lucy's life, win the contest, and prove yourself a major heroine, girl," said Terry. "Me and Lucy were ready to spank your bottom after you dragged that horndog panther back here last night, but now you're like, queen of the *X Dames*."

"Queen of the Dead's more like it," said Marcia. "God, I still can't believe what happened." Tears came into her eyes. "It was so surreal and scary. One minute it's a great contest, I was in a total groove, just dominating out there, and the next minute it's a nightmare at sea."

"Hey," said Lucy. "Be quiet a minute. I need to think." She sat up in bed, then put a hand to her forehead. "Oi, my head hurts. But some things are coming back to me now." She looked around. "Did you happen to save my camera along with me, Marcia?"

"I did. It's in your bag."

"Good job. Thanks." She stopped. "Now what I'm wondering is why would I pass out again for six hours if I was unconscious for like one or two minutes, or whatever, and then you brought me back. Is that normal?"

"What do you mean, normal?" Terry asked. "There's nothing normal about almost drowning, Luce."

"I know, I know, but still." She paused. "So where did they end up taking Sandra?"

"To the hospital in PV."

"Have they declared a cause of death?"

They both shrugged. "Not to us," said Terry. "In fact I can't say—at least not for sure—that she's dead. But we've been here keeping an eye on you since Marcia got her photo and video op collecting her prop winner's check from Judy and Bobby, who both smiled for the camera while Marcia looked like she was at a funeral."

"Well I was, kind of, wasn't I?" Marcia said.

"Yeah. You were," Terry said succinctly. "Then it was lunchtime. We weren't even remotely hungry so we borrowed a car and hauled you up here and haven't heard anything from anybody since."

"Poor Sandra," Lucy said. "She was a sweetheart, wasn't she? I mean, kinda tough, but really goodhearted. She just wanted to hang down here and spread the surf gospel. God damn." Lucy's eyes welled with tears. She wiped them with the edge of her bedsheet, and focused her still wavery brain: "Hey, listen, now that I'm up and OK, let's see if we can find out if they said yet how she died—and I'd like to see if we can get them to do a blood test on her, OK?"

"Whoa, Lucy, slow down. A blood test? Why?" asked Terry. "She drowned and got her head bashed in. Take your choice."

"Hey, you saved my ass and dragged me out of the water and woke me up and then I pass out for six hours. So what's up with that?" She looked at Marcia.

"What?"

"Sound like drugs to you?"

"Drugs? What do you mean, do you think I drugged her—and you?"

"No, not you, of course not. But maybe somebody did."

"But why?" Terry said. "What would be the point of—" It dawned on her. "What, one of the other competitors?"

"Moki Sue?" Marcia said. "No way. She was totally bummed out. That's half the reason I won. After what happened she could hardly paddle out, much less surf the way she needed to, to beat me. Same with Martina. As for me, I was pissed that they even continued with the contest, and I guess it's lucky for me that when I surf mad I surf really well. Comes from fighting the crowds at Malibu and Topanga, where you have to battle for every wave."

Lucy looked at her. "Listen, Marcia, I don't know how you surf when you're mad but I can tell you that I got a bunch of images of that first wave you got, when you did the aerial 360, and that was one spectacular maneuver, I have to say."

"Hey, thanks, Lucy. I've been working on that move but I never did it in a wave that big before. To tell the truth I don't know how I pulled it off."

"I'm pretty sure they got it on video, too," said Terry. "I could hear the judges barking about something totally awesome not long after the heat started."

"Video. Videotape!" cried Lucy. "That's it! We need to look at the videotape. From last night. From this morning. All of it. Every inch."

"For what?" Terry said. "Luce, Bobby's got all that stuff in the can already. He's scheduled a breakfast meet for nine a.m. tomorrow. Probably going to pack it in I would guess. What else can he do once everybody knows Sandra's died? If he wants to go on with the show he's got his episode, but it seems to me it would be in seriously bad taste."

"Bad taste? This is television we're talking about here! Do you really think he's going to cancel the show because of—"

"A death in the first week of shooting?! What else can he possibly do?"

Lucy looked at her. "You said it yourself, Ter. The guy's a sleaze. And we're talking about the Industry. This isn't going to stop him. If anything it'll inspire him to greater heights of sleaze."

Five minutes into the breakfast meeting the next day, Terry flashed a 'Girl you sure got that right' look at Lucy. Then they returned their attention to Bobby Schamberg, on his feet at the head of the long oval table, struggling to look gravely compassionate in light of the fact that he had just officially announced Sandra's death, by drowning and traumatic head injuries, to the entire cast and crew of *X Dames*, Episode One. Although the resemblance hadn't occurred to Lucy before that moment, the combination of false compassion and fake sincerity transparently layered atop shallow, selfish, scheming thoughtlessness made him look very much like one George W. Bush.

Lucy and Terry had taken a taxi to Bobby's house the night before. They had interrupted his intimate frolic involving two Canadian sisters and Henrietta; they had also interrupted a similar bit of business, it seemed, involving other characters, for even as they insisted to Bobby that he get his butt out of his overladen bed and let them have a look at the videotapes of the entire day's events, out of the corner of her eye through a window Lucy saw Judy Leggett and Ruben Dario skulking down a path towards the sea.

And then they'd watched the videotapes.

Things became subtly clear, at least to Lucy's suspicious eyes, as she viewed assorted fragments of unedited tape from the pre-contest breakfast on the veranda. First, Judy Leggett casually steered Sandra down to the end of the table, so that she ended up seated next to Lucy. Then Judy Leggett and Ruben Dario ran the waiters, keeping the food and drink coming, and at one point, a waiter with a pot was about to pour coffee for Lucy and Sandra when Judy sharply called him back. He went to her side, she spoke a few words to him, and then he returned to the kitchen, leaving the coffee pot on the table. Judy glanced around, picked up the coffee pot, and moved it out of sight under the lip of the table for just a few seconds. Then she put it back on the table. A moment later the same waiter came to the table, picked up the pot, and proceeded to head straight to the end of the table to pour coffee for Lucy and Sandra.

Lucy had kept her mouth shut, watching that tape. Then they'd watched some more tape, of the contest, and there was nothing odd to be seen. Later, she'd told Teresa what she thought. Teresa, who had watched with her, hadn't even noticed any of the business with the coffee pot.

Now they were in the midst of another breakfast on the veranda. As always, the camera guys were armed and shooting. Bobby cleared his throat. "My friends, I have an announcement to make which may strike some of you as strange, but this is the television business and sometimes things don't go exactly the way you expect them to. In light of Sandra Darwin's shocking accident and tragic demise, we have had to rethink certain elements of our show. Yesterday afternoon, one of our producers"—he glanced at Teresa—"called the Puerto Vallarta hospital where Sandra Darwin had been taken, and where she sadly, subsequently passed away. And this producer spoke with one of the doctors, and requested that they perform a blood test on Sandra, to see if there were any drugs involved. When I heard this I thought she meant steroids, but no, what she was talking about was—barbiturates, or opiates. This producer for some reason seemed to think that Sandra had been drugged prior to the contest, and that somehow these drugs had caused the accident—accidents—that led to her death. I think personally that she is crazy, this producer, but in the interests of making sure that we left no stone unturned regarding Sandra's demise, I informed Señor Dario—who is not here, by the way, because he is handling matters relating to Sandra's death for her family back home in Utah—that he should permit the doctor to obtain some of Sandra's blood prior to the embalming or cremation of her remains. However, Dario called me back an hour later and said that she had already been identified and sent to the mortuary for embalming, per her parents' request. And so this blood sample was unavailable."

"Wait a minute," said Lucy, standing. "You can't tell me that her body was embalmed on the same day as—"

"I'm afraid so, Ms. Ripken," said Bobby. "Señor Dario said that—"

"I don't care what Dario said. Don't you know why Teresa requested this?"

"I think I do, Lucy. Drugs, like I said."

"Yes, but what does the presence of such drugs in her body—the possible presence, I mean—tell you?"

"Nothing. I mean, what, that she had a drug problem?"

"No, of course not. Jesus, Bobby, why don't you try thinking—for once! Has it occurred to you that maybe she was drugged! That someone did it to her so she would drown during the contest, fool." The table buzzed.

"You want to keep your job, mind your manners, Lucy," Bobby said, but the way his nostrils flared, she could tell this public verbal combat was getting him off.

"Don't talk to me about manners, Bobby. We're talking about murder here."

"Murder? What the hell do you mean? You saw that waverunner land on her head, Lucy."

"But you said she died from drowning."

"And blunt force head trauma."

"Well guess what, Bob?"

"What?"

She paused dramatically. "For reasons which I will make obvious later, I had a sample of my own blood drawn last night, and rushed to the lab in PV. I had my own blood tested for opiates and barbiturates too. They called me with results early this morning. It appears that at some point yesterday I had been given a rather large dose of Seconal." A general outcry arose around the table. "You know what Seconal is, Bobby?"

"Of course I know what Seconal is. Every red-blooded American knows what Seconal is."

"Well all I have to say to you is," and Lucy stared directly at Judy Leggett, wearing shades, seated next to Bobby, "Have a look at your tape from yesterday's breakfast meeting." With that she sat down.

"What is she talking about?" Moki Sue demanded. "What the hell's going on?"

"Hey, hey, I don't know. Jesus," Bobby said. "Listen people, what I was going to tell you is that we have to stick around for a day or two, sort out the aftereffects of the tragedy, and see what we want to do next for the show. And then its on to Chile for the snowboarding competition. But meanwhile I intend to look into these—ah, interesting questions that have been raised by Ms. Ripken. I would like you all to meet me at Don Pedro's for lunch, at which time we'll have a new schedule. People, I know this has been something of a shocker, but we have to look at the big picture, don't we? And the truth is, for a lot of reasons we had an incredibly dramatic surfing contest yesterday. Lucy, Terry, can you guys come back to the house with me?"

"I'm coming too," Judy said, jumping up.

"Me too," said Marcia.

"Hey, I want to see what she's talking about," said Moki Sue.

"Yeah, we all do, Bobby," Charlene chimed in.

And so the remaining contestants, along with crew members and a few hangers on, climbed into the small fleet of rented SUVs for the short trip from the Villa Roma to La Casa de la Luna Grande.

They arrived at the house five minutes later, camera guys shooting as always. They entered to find Ruben Dario seated on a sofa talking on the phone. He held up a hand authoritatively, and the crowd hesitated in the foyer as he murmured into the phone. "Yes. OK, Mrs. Darwin. Yes. To-morrow. That's fine. Bye now." He hung up. "OK. Sorry. That's done. I'm shipping the body home tomorrow." He looked appropriately grave. "But hello, my friends. What are you all here for?"

"Videotape, Ruben," said Bobby. "We need to look at the tape from yesterday's breakfast."

"Well you have all that on the machine in your room, do you not, Señor Bobby?"

"Yes I do. Please wait here folks." He walked down a long hallway while fourteen people filled the living room, dominated by a massive television monitor at one end. A couple of digital editing machines sat on a table nearby. Bobby emerged a minute later with a disc that had the words "pre-con breakfast" scrawled on one side. He put it in one of the machines, cued it up, and ran it.

They all watched. The DVD ran through the breakfast. Lucy was dumbfounded: the bits that she'd identified as suspicious had been seamlessly erased. Nothing showed how she and Sandra had been herded to one end; nothing about the waiter and the coffee pot and Judy Leggett. They were simply gone. It ended. Bobby looked at Lucy. They all did. "Lucy," said Bobby. "Was there something on there that . . . did I . . . did we miss something?"

"No. I mean yes. I mean I don't know," Lucy said, flustered. Teresa put a hand on her arm, and gave her a look.

"Hey, Lucy did take barbiturates yesterday, and she doesn't know how. So maybe she didn't recall exactly what—"

"I know what I saw, dammit, Terry."

"I know Lucy," she murmured. "Just be cool."

"Well, in any case," said Bobby. "I don't see any reason for you all to hang around here. I would suggest you all go to the beach, enjoy those little waves out there—thank god that monster swell is over, eh?—and we'll get together for lunch like I said. Lucy, Terry," he added, "can you two stick around for a few minutes?"

"Here comes the shaft," Terry said to Lucy. "Any last words?"

They waited while the gang filed out. Ruben Dario lingered, arrogant dark eyes on Lucy—and then he left as well.

"Well, ladies," Bobby said. "Want a coffee?"

"I have a copy of that DVD," Teresa said quietly.

"What?" Bobby said.

"I came back here and copied it on my computer last night, when you guys were all down at Don Pedro's 'mourning' Sandra's demise with all those margaritas. Don't even think about getting mad, Bobby," she added quickly, as Schamberg puffed himself up. "You have zero credibility here. But I will say that I know you would never have anything to do with what happened out there, and that's why I'm letting you in on this."

"Thanks, I guess," said Bobby. "But what's the point? There's nothing on that tape that says anything, Terry. Which brings me to my next point. I'm thinking that maybe—well, we're not sure exactly when the—"

"Bobby, be quiet a minute, will you?" Terry said. "I know you're ready to fire Lucy and me, but first I want you to remember what you just saw, and then look at this." She took a DVD out of her purse and slid it into the machine. After a few seconds, the same video they'd just watched started up. But then, at a certain point, something else showed up: Judy herding Lucy and Sandra down the table. They watched some more, and soon saw the incident with the coffee pot and the waiter. This time, Lucy noted, when the waiter came back from the kitchen he gave Judy a cigarette—that's what she'd sent him to fetch, it seems— which she lit, and smoked, they saw in snatched bits, as she watched him deliver the coffee to Lucy and Sandra's cups at the other end of the table.

"And so?" Bobby asked impatiently when it ended.

"Did you see anything different?"

"Yeah. Judy seating you guys and then getting the guy to get her a cigarette."

"Did you see the coffee pot disappear?"

"She poured coffee into her cup in her other hand. Jesus, this—"

"Her cup's on the table, Bobby. She's putting something in the pot down there. She's—"

"This is the most paranoid thing I've—"

"Then why did Ruben just edit it out of the tape we all watched, Bobby?" Lucy said. "Can't you see what's happening?"

He shook his head. "You two are fucking nuts. How do you know Ruben did that? What are you saying? That Judy—Judy and Ruben tried to have—that they drugged and murdered Sandra? But why? What the hell for?"

"They also drugged me, Bobby," Lucy said. "And I have no clue as to why. Do you?"

"What do you think?" he snapped. "Why the fuck would anyone want to drug a writer?" he sneered. "All you have to do is fire them."

"Fuck you, Bobby," Terry said. "Can't you see this is serious?"

"Whatever." He shrugged. "So what do you want to do, ladies? My suggestion is you shut the hell up about all this paranoid conjecture and take the next plane home to LA. I'll be happy to pay you a month—two months!—salary to ease the pain, if that's what you're looking for."

"Whoa, Bobby boy," said Teresa. "Don't get condescending on me. Besides, I have a better idea, if you don't mind listening for five minutes."

"What would that be, Terry?" he said dismissively. He'd already written them out of his script.

Lucy took the reins. She and Terry had worked it out earlier, after getting Lucy's blood work back and watching the video one more time. The whole scene they'd just played out had been an act, to get the guilty parties to let down their guard. "Get the cast and crew comfortable with the idea of sticking around a few days to shoot more background, location, other footage to fill in. That should be easy enough, since you already mentioned a day or two of downtime. Meanwhile, Terry and Marcia and I can look into this a little further. We have some leads we're working on. Just let us have Mary and one of your cameramen— that guy Hector Valdez would be my choice, because he speaks Spanish fluently—to shoot everything we find. Then if we get something good, you can incorporate it into the show as a real-life murder mystery, solved in real time. I don't know what could kick off a new TV show better than a real murder, with real people solving it, as a part of a show about a real-life surfing contest. We don't even have to involve the cops if we find something out, unless you want us to write it that way. It will be a first, man. It'll make the show."

Terry finished: "And if we can't figure anything out or we're just being paranoid, you've still got your surfing contest with a built-in tragedy, and then you're off to Chile."

He stared at them, and then a smile broke out on his face. "Fuck, MacDonald, you are such a genius. God damn!" He looked at his watch. "Three days. Make it happen. I'll cover your asses and keep everybody busy."

"Including Ruben Dario—and Judy," Terry added ominously.

He looked concerned. "Yeah. I guess she's a—what would you call her?"

"A Person of Interest," said Lucy. "That's one notch below 'suspect.'"

"Right," he said. "Well, I'd better get back to the beach and see what's up." He headed out.

"Good job, Terry," said Lucy. They high-fived. "Good job, Luce," Terry said. They low-fived. "So now what?"

"Pharmacies. Internet. Real estate. That's where we want to go. I think you and Marcia and the camera guy Hector Valdez should work south from here towards PV, find the pharmacies, and see if you can find out anything about any prescriptions Judy or anyone connected to her might have gotten. I think we can clue Valdez in, and he can translate for you and shoot anything that happens. I'm going to sit Miss Mary Miles down and tell her what's up—I know she's got nothing to do with this, and she can shoot me with that little handheld camcorder she's been using. I want to see what I can find out about Dario and Townsend, without showing my hand. I'll also check in with some friends via phone and email to see if we can do a little hacking into the Realtors' office Web site. That may be the best way to see what's up with those guys."

7

Dope and Paranoia

After Marcia and Terry left to meet Hector Valdez, Lucy fished out her camera and was just about to turn it on and review her images when she stopped and put it down. Time for a moment of reflection. She put her head in her hands, elbows on the desk, and sighed. Then she looked out at the ocean, where two-foot-high waves broke close to shore. The swell had completely disappeared.

It had been only four days since she and Harold said their goodbyes at LaGuardia. What an insane week! She needed to hear from him, even if he was buried in the Florida mud on his mad tunneling mission. She needed to tell him what was up, see what he had to say. Harold had sharp insights into these criminal situations, and even when they were oceans or continents apart, Lucy never hesitated to pick his brains if the opportunity arose. And to rip his pants off when the oceans between them went away. She missed him. Damn did she miss him right now.

And she needed to check in with Jane in the building, see where the deal with the landlord had gotten itself to; she also needed to talk to her pal Mickey, who had a friend she swore could hack into any computer in the world from his fifth-floor walkup railroad flat on East 9th Street.

Five minutes to noon. She watched Mary strolling up the road towards the hotel. Harold, Jane, and Mickey's hacker would have to wait. At least her dog was doing well. Earlier Marcia had called her sis, and Mariah reported that Claud had learned how to bodysurf and had befriended no fewer than six of the neighborhood hounds.

"Hey, what's up?" Lucy went out on her veranda to greet Mary.

"Hi, Lucy," she said. "How are you feeling?"

"Me? I'm fine."

"I mean after your accident yesterday."

"Mary, that was no accident. Trust me on this. But I'm over it regardless. Sit down. You want some coffee?"

"No, I'm good." They sat at the patio table. "So what did you want to talk about here? I think we've gotten this thing—well, I'm not sure if 'wrapped' is the right word, but I've got enough footage to make the first episode work, one way or another. I'm looking forward to some cooler weather. Believe it or not I kick ass on a snowboard."

"I believe it. Those twenty-five-year-olds got nothin' on you." She paused. "Listen, Mary, I've seen you casting a skeptical eye Bobby's way more than once. And I think you know, or at least sense, that something weird happened yesterday." She waited. So did Mary. Lucy bit the bullet. "Can I show you something?"

"Sure."

She opened the laptop and ran the unedited footage for her, pausing it here and there to explain what was up with Judy and the coffee, and how those parts had disappeared from the original. Then she told her the plan she and Terry had sold to Bobby.

"And he's going for it?" Mary asked incredulously. "Even though you told him Judy is involved?"

"Hey, it's showbiz. And this is a real mystery, because we simply can not figure out why they went after me too. I think—I don't know—that Sandra's death has something to do with Judy being so tight with Henrietta, that there was something going on with rigging the contest. Not that Bobby knew anything, he's clueless. But why me?"

"Just an accident, Lucy. You were sitting next to her, you got coffee at the same time. Assuming that your entire thesis has any basis in reality."

"Oh, I don't doubt that it does. But why would Judy let him pour me a cup of coffee, knowing it would knock me out, knowing that I would be obviously drugged and at least indirectly give away their plans? Why didn't Judy just stop him after he'd poured Sandra's coffee? It would have been easy to do."

She pondered. "Good question. Maybe Judy just doesn't like your looks. I've known her a few years and she's one of the prettiest cutthroats in Hollywood, I will say. Or maybe they just guessed you were going out there to shoot, knowing what a gung ho girl you're rumored to be, and they did it just to get you out of the way, either in the water or before you paddled out. Did you mention to anyone that you planned to go out in the waves to shoot stills?"

"Only Marcia, because I needed to borrow her long-board. And I know she's not in on this since she's the one who saved my ass."

"Seems like somebody must have figured it out. What do you think?"

"I just don't know. Terry's working on the drug angle, to see if we can trace the barbies. But somewhere down the line we'll figure out the reasons they came after Sandra, and after me. That I will guarantee you. Look, this is all material, right? And you need material. Mary, you know this is going to be a really hot property if we've happened on to a real-life murder." She gave her best conspiratorial grin. "So I was hoping you'd shoot my part of the investigation with your camcorder, and then we can include it in the episode, or movie, or whatever this turns out to be. And use it for evidence if necessary."

Mary grinned. "I have to say that you and your pal Teresa have come up with one of the more audacious ideas I've seen in play of late, and with this ridiculous reality TV boom Hollywood is full of weird shit these days."

"Just imagine the ratings if we actually bust somebody and solve a murder on the show."

"So let's roll, baby. I've got my camcorder right here in my bag." She pulled it out, pointed it at Lucy, and turned it on. She narrated. "Here we have Lucy Ripken, book writer turned TV writer turned sleuth, attempting to discover if and how our surfer-girl contest entrant Sandra Darwin was murdered. This, friends, is director Mary Miles, and we are beginning act two of episode one of the *X Dames*. In act one, Marcia Hobgood, a twenty-three-year-old nonprofessional from Venice, California, came out of nowhere to win the *X Dames* surfing contest over several seasoned pros, but during the contest as you know, Sandra Darwin, favored by some to take home the first *X Dames* prize, died under what Ms. Ripken claims are suspicious circumstances. And how do you propose to solve this mysterious crime, Lucy Ripken?"

Lucy smiled awkwardly. "At the moment I need to make a couple of phone calls to New York, so you can turn that thing off."

"I don't think so, Lucy," said Mary. "I don't want to miss anything, know what I mean? And you asked for it."

"Fine, fine," Lucy said. She got on the phone, got a dial tone, and punched in Harold's cell number. It rang about six times and then his voicemail took the call.

"Harold here. Spare me all but the details. Later."

"Hey Harry, it's Lucy in Sayulita. How's your dig doing? Hope you found the mother lode. Meanwhile I've gotten myself into another predicament down here. I need to talk to you. Try my cell, but its spotty. I'm in suite five at the Villa Roma Hotel." She gave him the number and hung up, then looked at the camera. "That was exciting, eh?"

"You want to say anything about Harold? Like, who is he?"

"None of your business," Lucy said.

"Fine, fine," Mary laughed. "Who's next?"

"My neighbor, Jane Aronstein, who lives downstairs from me in SoHo, New York. She's been looking out for my loft while I'm gone. I'm just calling to check on it, OK? You want to turn off your machine?"

"No way, Lucy," Mary said. "You haven't watched much TV, have you? We need all this backstory—to fill in the blanks—and to fill the time, kiddo. Just pretend I'm not here."

Four hours later, Lucy put a lid on her anxiety as they began their meeting. And she had to admit to herself that Mary was a prescient girl. She'd gotten some undeniably interesting footage of Lucy on the phone with various players, and caught her mood as it spiraled down through disbelief and on into paranoid shock and rage.

But first came the report from Terry and Marcia, accompanied by a ton of good footage shot by Hector Valdez. Terry did the voice-over as they gathered round to watch the DVD on her laptop. "Hector said the nearest pharmacies are in Bucerias, which is about halfway back to Puerto Vallarta, on the other side of the hill. So here we are getting in the car, blah blah blah, leaving Sayu, heading through the forest. Enough of this already. Now, Bucerias. There's the first *farmacia*—that big white building with the red cross at the side of the road. So we parked and went in and Hector asked if he could get a bottle of Seconal or a bottle of Valium or codeine. The pharmacist is saying no, you must have a prescription. Then Hector in Spanish is asking where is the doctor who will give this prescription, and you can see the pharmacist shrug, and say *no se*, I don't know.

"So it's off, on foot, in search of the *farmacia sleazaria*, down the street here. We wandered around a bit—it's kind of a shabby but colorful little town—and ended up by the beach, where we found this seafood place that Hector had said was really good. So we had lunch. I know, I know, not part of the story, but wait, it gets better." They viewed footage of the town and restaurant and the women vamping over some platters of food, then they moved back onto the street and unseen Hector taped from behind as Terry and Marcia spotted another *farmacia* on a quieter side street. On screen the two women walked in and approached the woman behind the counter. Marcia in broken Spanish and with mime indicated that she was in very much pain and could they help her. The woman offered Advil, and Marcia said, *no gracias*, do you have *mucho* stronger pills please. The woman shook her head, said you need a prescription, speaking in English, and then she said, you must go and see Doctor Luis Cardozo, he is in the clinic two blocks down upstairs on the left side of the road. *Muchas gracias*, etc. They went out, and walked down the street, and soon found a sign that said *Clinica, open 8 a.m.–8 p.m., Doctor Luis Cardozo*. They went in, Hector still shooting from behind, and up a dingy flight of stairs to find a small waiting room. Behind a window, the receptionist was a well-groomed, pretty young thing. This time Terry approached, and asked about a consultation. The woman looked at the camera and slightly frowned but then said, what is the problem? Terry said *migrano in mi cabeza*, tapping her temple and grimacing, and apparently the woman got it. Speaking broken English and looking at her watch, she said a consultation is twenty-five dollars. Terry asked can I get a prescription? She said no problem. The doctor is in. But you can not take that in, she said, looking at the camera. *No problema*, Terry said, sitting down, then getting up to go in to see the doctor.

Jump cut to Terry coming out. She looked right at the camera. "So this is the deal: I went in there and I said I had a migraine—this Doctor Cardozo speaks English perfectly well—and asked could he help me. He said, what would you like? I said, some sort of pain pill. He said I will prescribe OxyContin, it is very effective. And also, I said, I have had some trouble sleeping because of it, and he said, I can also prescribe Valium or Ambien if you are willing to pay the consultation fee. I said sure, I was almost laughing at him by now, but he didn't care. I gave him the money, five hundred pesos, and then said, Oh, by the way, I almost forgot, my friend Judy Leggett up in Sayulita needs a refill on her prescription. She's really sick today and couldn't make the trip down. He looked at me, then looked in his drawer, and pulled out a scrip pad. He wrote me two prescriptions, then thumbed through the pink second sheets of scrips he'd already written. Then he became all apologetic, and said, I am sorry but I wrote her Seconal and OxyContin prescriptions and gave them to Señor Dario only five days ago, and since there were twenty doses in each I can not write another one for her until, let me see . . . he looked at his calendar . . . next Wednesday at the very soonest. However, with extenuating circumstances this delay can be circumvented if you are willing to pay double the required consultation fee in advance, as I may write this up as a medical emergency therefore justifying the need for . . . "

"God, he's Doctor Feelgood," Lucy cut in. Terry paused the DVD.

"No shit. And we sure as hell know where Judy got her drugs. Oxy for herself, and Seconal for you and Sandra. She and Dario didn't even try to cover their tracks. The arrogant fools."

"Did you get copies of those scrips?" Mary asked. "It might help to have them."

"No. I asked, but he wouldn't do it," Terry said. "And he wouldn't let us film him, understandably. I should have been tape recording but I didn't think to bring one down. But we do have the prescriptions he wrote for me—anybody wants any dope I can get it for them," she laughed, "which we might be able to use somehow or other. At least to get the good doctor into the story. We thought of sticking around and doing a sneak attack on him with the camcorder when he came out of his office but it seemed cruel. He's just a hack making money off the bad habits of gringos on vacation. It hardly seems worth it to ruin him. His involvement in this is unwitting I'm sure."

"I guess," said Lucy. "But he's sure loose with that prescription pad."

"There's a long tradition of that here, Lucy. People have come to Mexico to cop cheap drugs for decades," Mary said. "Guys like Cardozo are simply meeting a need."

"No shit," said Marcia. "I have friends who go to Tijuana for Valium, codeine, and birth control pills, and my mom gets her Retin-A and Ambien down there."

"Well, you guys certainly made some serious progress," Lucy said. "I wish I could say the same." She sighed. It was her turn now. She had enjoyed the last few minutes, when her mind was on matters other than what was going on in New York.

"What about you, Lucy? What happened up here with—"

"It's a nightmare."

"What are you talking about?"

"I'm still in shock. That's why I let you guys do your thing first. I meant to get down to the real estate office but I got sidetracked. Mary, you want to run this bummer?"

"OK, Luce, if it's all right with you." She popped out the DVD and put in another. They ran through Lucy's intro and the first phone call, to Harold's cell. Then, on screen, Lucy looked at the camera and said, "OK, OK, keep it rolling, Mary. Invade my universe, I don't care. Here's the story: right now I'm calling my neighbor in New York, Jane Aronstein, to check on my loft. This has nothing to do with our investigation but Mary insisted on shooting it anyways." She punched in a bunch of numbers, and waited. Off-screen, Mary said to Lucy, "I can turn this into a speaker phone. Do you mind?"

Lucy remembered her first impulse was to say, hell, yes, I mind but then, instead, she shrugged. "No. Go ahead."

They all watched the computer screen, where Lucy now talked on the phone. "Hey Jane, how are you? It's Lucy."

Jane came through muffled but understandable on the speaker phone. "I'm good, Lucy. Hey, how's the weather in LA?"

"LA? I don't—oh, of course. I'm in Mexico, Janey. I came down like two days after I got to LA. We're working on the show down here."

"Mexico? Cool. How's the weather?"

"It's great. So's everything OK with the loft? Has Lascovich been around?"

"No. But your friend came by the other day and got the keys."

"My friend? What friend? What are you talking about?" Lucy, on screen, looked shocked and dismayed.

"Mickey. Your writer friend, the one you said you went to Jamaica with a couple of years ago. I remembered her name since there aren't many girls named Mickey. She said she'd talked to you and you told her it was OK if she stayed there while she was getting a new kitchen put into her apartment on Roosevelt Island. She said you'd called from LA, that the *X Dames* show was going great, and that you thought you'd be out there staying with your friend Terry for a while. She obviously knew you so I gave her the keys."

"Jesus." Lucy held the phone, her uncertainty emanating from the screen. "Jane, I thought we agreed you weren't going to give the keys to anyone but me."

"I know, I know, you're worried about Lascovich. But he's not even around. He and his wife went to Florida. They left the day after you did."

"So Mickey's up there now?"

"I guess. You want me to go knock on the door?"

"No. Forget about it. I'll call her. But I wish you'd checked with me."

"Lucy, I tried your cell. It wasn't working. She was really nice, and said all the right things, so—"

"OK, OK. I'm not blaming you. I just—oh, never mind. Hey, what did this woman look like?"

"I don't know. I mean I was in the middle of something so I wasn't really paying attention. Let me think. She had long, wavy blonde hair, she was probably in her late thirties or early forties, she wore spectacles, and she was dressed in sort of nouveau hippie clothes but expensively, it seems to me. She seemed fashion-conscious. I remember thinking she was really skinny."

"Hmm." Lucy couldn't picture anyone she knew. She especially couldn't picture mouse-haired, wide-bottomed Mickey. "Well, I guess I'll see you when I see you, Jane." She hung up. "Damn." She looked into the camera. "Lascovich is messing with me here, I think."

Mary, offscreen, said, "You want to fill us in?"

"Not right now. I've got to make another call this minute." She picked up the phone and punched in a bunch of numbers.

"Hello?" The speaker phone was still on.

"Hey, Mick, is that you?"

"Yes, who's this?"

"It's me. Lucy Ripken."

"Hey, Luce, sorry I didn't recognize your voice. This cell phone sucks. I was just thinking about you this very morning. I heard something about—"

"So you're not in my loft?"

"What? Why would I be in your loft?"

"You didn't call my downstairs neighbor Jane, get my new keys, and move into my loft while your kitchen's being remodeled?"

"What are you talking about, Lucy? I'm sitting in my apartment on Roosevelt Island, gazing longingly at TV commercials for bad food while eating carrot sticks by the hundreds. I'm down to one hundred thirty eight point six pounds and still on it."

"That's great," Lucy said into the phone, then looked directly at the camera. "What the hell's going on?"

"Lucy, what are you talking about?"

"Mick, here's the deal: I'm in Mexico working on this TV show and somebody posing as you got the keys to my place and got in. She knew enough about me to convince my neighbor that she was you. That's all I know. I don't know who or why or what but I suspect the landlord is up to something."

"God damn, that's pretty weird. Do you want me to go and see what's up?"

"No, no, I don't think you should stick your nose into this."

"But if someone gets legal possession you'll never get back in there."

"I know," Lucy said. "I'm in a total bind. But I heard my landlord's out of town for a week, so maybe I'll beat him back and then—we'll see. Meanwhile, I'm like five thousand miles away. Damn! Ain't life a bitch. Well, listen I have one other thing I wanted to ask you."

"Anything for you, Luce. You want me to go shoot this broad, get the keys back?"

"Yeah, I'll pay you five hundred bucks for the hit. No, seriously, once upon a time you told me you knew this guy in the East Village who was like the best computer hacker in the known universe."

"Slope Tweed."

"Slope Tweed?"

"That's his name. He's still there, on East Ninth. Completely wacko, but yes, he's the best hacker I've ever met, known, or heard of, and he loves me madly so he will do your bidding if I tell him to do so."

"I might need him."

"You might?"

"Yeah. I have some things I'm looking into and I might have to hack into some email and some other stuff on a Web site down here."

"Down where?"

"I'm in this little town near Puerto Vallarta, and somebody got killed."

"Jesus, Lucy, are you in the middle of another one of your escapades? I still tell people about our adventures solving the death of Awful Angus down in Ochi."

"Yep, I'm at it again. And once again it came out of nowhere."

"You're lucky that way. New material just falls in your lap. Ha! Well, anyway, here's his number." Lucy wrote it down. "I'll call him after we get off the phone and tell him Lucy Ripken calls, do what she asks."

"Muchas Gracias, Señorita Mickita."

"My pleasure. And Lucy?"

"Yeah Mick."

"Do me a favor and watch your ass."

"Will do, Mick."

"Let me know when you want to do the hit on the loft impostor. We only need one Mickey Wolfe in the world and that's me."

"Right on, Mick. See ya." They both hung up.

"So someone hijacked your loft?" Terry said. "What a bummer."

"You have no idea what a bummer, if that is what happened. My landlord is a hound from hell and it smells like he's behind this," Lucy said. "In any case, that's all I got done today," she said. "It was—upsetting."

"I can imagine," Mary said. "Listen, tomorrow we'll check out the real estate office. I'll shoot with the mini-cam and see what shakes. After that, we'll use your friend's pal if we need to. Slope Tweed, huh? Sounds like an interesting specimen." Mary was seriously into it now, Lucy could tell. Smelling blood.

"All I can tell you guys is we have to get this done fast because I have got to get back to New York ASAP," Lucy said. "I don't know what's up with the *X Dames* but I am not going to lose that place for any stinking TV show."

"So let's get on it," said Terry. "Marcia, you go with Mary to see that Townsend dolt in Dario's office tomorrow. Tell him you want to invest your *X Dames* winnings in a Sayulita surf hut. Mary's your financial advisor or whatever."

They left Lucy alone. After a room service dinner she began to get into a major fret about her loft again, trying to figure out how to take it back from afar. Nothing seemed feasible. Then the phone rang. She pounced on it.

"Lucy here."

"Hey Luce, it's me." Harold.

"Damn am I glad to hear your voice," she said. "Things have gotten really weird, Harry. Are you still in Florida? How's it going down there? You strike it rich yet?"

"Whoa, Lucy, slow down. Things are OK. Moving. Remember my friend Prudence in Jamaica? Well, I called her and she hooked me up with these two cousins of hers who've been working as cane-cutters on some rich-ass exile Cuban's plantation about two hours from here. So I tracked them down and when I told them I was a friend of cousin Prudence they got really friendly. They bailed on their cane-cutting gigs—God, that's ugly, hard, shit-paying work—but anyways, they were very happy to help me start digging for twenty-five-bucks an hour against ten percent of my haul. I don't believe they think we're going to find bags of money, and the ground is pretty damp, but—"

"Harry, cut to the chase. Are you there?"

"We're about fifty feet into it. I found a maintenance guy to get me plans to help me steer around some plumbing so that took a little extra time and payola. We can only work midnight to five a.m. and I also had to invest some time in shoring things up because the ground's so damp. All in all, it's taking a little longer than I thought. But another three days or so we'll be there. Say a little prayer for me, Lucy. Now that I'm actually doing this it seems pretty preposterous I must admit."

"But you don't want to cut your losses and get back to New York, huh?"

"No way, Luce. I got a serious tunnel going here, and I'm way too close to my target at this point. Why? What's up?"

"Someone's in my loft since yesterday and I don't know who."

"What?"

Lucy told him the story. "So here I am in Sayulita and the mysterious stranger has moved into my place. I figure Lascovich is behind this but on the other hand I don't know how he could find out about the *X Dames* gig, which this woman used to trick Jane and get in, so I'm also thinking it might be someone connected to somebody on the show because she knew all about it."

"But you told Lascovich you were leaving, right? So he found out where you were going and—hey, how is that going? The show I mean."

"Murder and mayhem on the high waves, what else?"

"What?"

She told him another story.

"Jesus, Luce, you are so good at stepping into it. So what are you going to do?"

"Oh, we have a plan, don't worry. If things go right, Teresa and I are going to turn this lurid scenario into the TV event of the next fall season. Surfing is a hot ticket right now, Harry. And murder always sells. So put 'em together and what do you got? Bibble te bobble te boo. A Nielsen sweep. But it will probably take a few days to pull it off so I was hoping you might make it back to Manhattan before Lascovich gets back and see if you could get rid of this person in my loft."

"And how am I supposed to accomplish that?"

"Harold, you are one wily character when you need to be."

"I guess that's a compliment, but I still need a couple of days to unearth my million."

"Still think it's there, huh?"

"I sure as hell can't walk away without knowing one way or the other. I'll be back in New York, let me see, today's Tuesday—Saturday afternoon, I would guess."

"I think Lascovich will be back in his office on Monday."

"I'll check it out Saturday night or Sunday, see what's up. But damn. Lucy, it's Manhattan real estate. People kill for that much space. You know the deal." She didn't respond. "I'll do what I can."

"Thanks, Harry." She paused, and softened her voice. "And Harry?"

He knew that tone. "Yes, Lucy?" he said slowly, drawing it out, and she could picture him smiling his patented, come hither and strip—immediately if not sooner—smile.

"You know what I want to do to you next time I see you, Harry?"

"I have a pretty good idea, Luce," he said. "And I'm sure you know that I eagerly await your ministrations. Or as the man once said, I could use a lemon-squeezer."

"I only hope that it is in my own bed, in my loft, that we can make lemonade."

"I'll see what I can do, baby."

Aaah, that was a nice closer, she thought, putting down the phone. A little bit of Harry, even from afar by phone, went a long way at a time like this.

8

A Rotten Deal and an Email Trail

At ten o'clock the next morning, accompanied by Mary with her mini-cam hidden in her bag, the new *X Dames* surfing champion Marcia Hobgood wandered into the office of Sayulita Development Company and asked to speak with Ruben Dario. Dario had gone to Puerto Vallarta, according to snarky, self-important Violeta, sexy young high-heeled office manager, and so they met with Wally Townsend instead. Lucy knocked back a fresh carrot, celery, and ginger juice while waiting in El Juicy Internet Café across the street, watching. Lucy had sent an email to Slope Tweed at seven a.m., before her surfing lesson with Marcia commenced. She'd ridden six waist-high waves, done a couple of decent bottom turns, and even shuffled up and tried a little nose-riding. Now it was down to business.

Fifteen minutes after entering the office, the two women emerged with Townsend. He was around fifty, a heavy-set white guy with a permanent terra cotta tan, thinning slicked-back hair, and a taste for gaudy Hawaiian shirts. He'd been around all week, but seemed a marginal character, the resident gringo knucklehead in the plot as it developed thus far. Now they were going to use him.

The three of them climbed into a red SUV and drove off. Lucy jumped onto her borrowed-from-the-hotel, fat-tired beach bicycle and followed them up the street, eating dust all the way. They went halfway around the plaza, turned right, and headed down a narrow side street jammed with parked cars. Three blocks later they stopped. Lucy caught up to them just as Townsend unlocked a gate and they stepped into a property hidden behind a high white wall.

They went in. She waited a minute, then approached the gate. It let into a lush, beautifully landscaped yard, with myriad fruit trees, flowering shrubs, and small fountains. Flowing water and birds made sweet, soothing sounds, and butterflies fluttered amidst the flowers. A stone path led through the secret glade to a charming little one-story white stucco house with a red tile roof and a small covered veranda: a tiny jewel of a dwelling, in perfect condition. The lushly planted grounds extended around both sides of the building, and seemed to go on beyond it for quite a ways. Lucy had a quick look around the yard, then dodged out the gate as Townsend emerged from the house with Marcia and Mary. Lucy jumped on her bike, waited, then followed them back down the road. They returned to the realty office and after a few moments the two women came out. They gathered at the Internet café.

Mary started. "I don't think Townsend was in on it, since he seems so utterly amazed at his own good fortune that he can hardly contain himself."

"In on what? What do you mean?" Lucy asked.

"That was Sandra Darwin's house," Marcia said grimly. "She had just recently bought it, in partnership with Dario and Townsend. And now they're going to tear down that beautiful house and rip up all those trees and flowers and build a three-story fourteen-unit condominium project on the site. Townsend thought maybe I wanted to put my twenty-five grand in prize money as a 10 percent deposit on a pre-build price of two hundred and fifty thousand dollars for a two-bedroom unit, possibly with a territorial view. He's sure I'll be able to double my money once they get the plans in place and start marketing the units. Even better I don't take the money across the border I don't pay taxes. Yadda yadda yadda. It was an offer I could refuse."

Lucy considered things. "I guess the question is where did Sandra fit into this deal? I know she was concerned about her living situation, but how was she involved?" she said. "We need to find out who was the seller and what were the terms."

"I asked Townsend already," Marcia said. "Just playing curious, you know? He said the seller had requested that they not reveal his name."

"Did he say why?"

"He said it was a matter of privacy."

"Hmm," said Lucy. "I think he's full of shit. Well, listen girls, I'm going to ride back up there and sniff around a bit, OK? I'll see you back at the suite later." They headed off to the beach while Lucy jumped on her bike and rode up to the property.

She went past the house, turned at the next corner, bounced down a bumpy little alley, and turned again. She rolled a few yards down the street, to where she would be directly behind the house—and here she discovered another pretty little house of about the same vintage, only this one did not have a wall around it. Instead, in a somewhat scruffy yard chickens pecked at the dirt, a trio of fat brown goats ate weeds, a single cow stood still, lines of laundry fluttered in the faint breeze, and three small boys dashed about underfoot. A Mexican woman roughly Lucy's age was taking shirts and underwear down from one of the clotheslines. Lucy approached. *"Buenos Días,"* she said.

"Hola," said the woman, and gave her a smile. "How are you?" she said in lightly accented English.

"You speak English?" Lucy said, a little surprised.

"Yes. I have been studying it with my friend, but she is—" she stopped, and her face fell.

"Your friend? You mean—" Intuiting, Lucy looked past her, and past her house, to where her yard flowed, unfenced, into what was clearly the backyard of the house beyond. Sandra's house.

"Sí. Yes. Sandra. I teach her Spanish, she teach me English. We were—like sisters. Friends for many years." She stopped again, obviously overcome.

"I'm sorry," Lucy said. "I have only just met her and she was a very good person. I feel very sad for her family, and her friends. But I wonder—I am trying to find out something about what happened to her, and—do you know who was the owner of the house there, that she lived in?"

"The owner? Yes, but of course. It is my father who owns that house and this, where I live with my family."

"Your father. Is he here? Could I speak with him?"

"He is fishing, like he is every day. He will be back in—" she looked up at the sun. "One hour more, maybe two."

"Does he speak English?"

"No, but I will help you talk with him. And my husband who is with him also speaks English a little bit like me."

"Your English is excellent," Lucy said. "I only wish my Spanish was this good. I hate not being able to talk to people in the street."

"Most of the Americans that come here do not wish to speak Spanish," she said, and shrugged. "So we all learn English."

"I seem to forget my Spanish as fast as I learn it," Lucy said. "But I keep trying."

"No problem, Miss—"

"Lucy. Lucy Ripken."

"And I am Mariela Pastor." They shook hands.

"Muchas Gracias, Mariela. See you later."

Lucy found Teresa and Mary sitting in a coffee shop on the plaza, fending off the chattery advances of a couple of shave-headed, ear-ringed, nipple-ringed, tongue-pierced, and heavily tattooed aging Dutch hippie men. They shooed the Dutchmen away and Lucy gave them the latest news. They then gave her theirs: they were scheming to turn the thing into a two-hour reality-based movie of the week. Mary thought she and Bobby might even get one of the broadcast networks to bite, if they could push the Outside Network into a second slot by guaranteeing them syndication rights if the series followed. The story was weird enough, she figured, in its evolution from reality-based women's sports competition to real-life murder mystery. If that's what it was. They sat for a minute, watching the tourists and locals wander by, mulling the decidedly strange, post-postmodern nature of what they were doing: investigating a crime while making a movie out of the investigation. Or was it a documentary at this point? A docudrama?

Then back into action. Lucy took Mary and her mini-cam with her on the second trip to Mariela's house, where she found her in the company of two men, a slender, well-built white-haired guy who looked to be pushing seventy, and a heavyset man of forty or so, with longish hair and a bandito's mustache. They sat on the porch steps gutting fish at high speed, and throwing the innards to a pair of small black dogs, who caught and gulped them down as fast as the men could throw them. Unable to resist, Mary turned on the camcorder and started shooting. The men stood, wiping their hands on blood-stained T-shirts and ragged cutoffs. Lucy and Mariela did the introductions, and Lucy then explained that they wanted to film the discussion. Mary kept filming. The men—Mariela's father was José Luís Caselin, and her husband was Pancho Pastor—wanted to know why. Lucy hesitated, and chose to be blunt. She explained, in English, that they were not sure that Sandra had died by accident and so they were looking into any reasons anyone would have to do her harm, and wanted to make a record of everything they discovered. Mariela quickly translated for her father, who said something back rapidly in Spanish. When he stopped, Mariela said, "You mean to say that you think someone caused her to die, yes? This is what my father asks."

"Yes," said Lucy. "That is what I think is possible."

"Why do you think this?" Mariela asked, and then turned to her father and spoke briefly. Her father, Señor José Luís Caselin, had seemed a taciturn man to that point. But now, with a determined look on his face, he began speaking, and as he worked his way into his argument he grew more animated and excited. Clearly he was getting something serious off his chest. It took him five minutes, a non-stop tirade. And then he fell silent and sat down, exhausted.

"He says many things, Lucy," Mariela said. "But in the end it is only one thing. I will try to make this clear for you. My father believes that our town is being stolen by people who care nothing for the people who have lived here for many years, and for those who would like to live in the old ways. And he thinks that what has happened here to us is part of that bigger story, so he tells the story of the house where Sandra lived, that has been in our family for almost fifty years. My father and my uncle León helped their father, my grandfather, built these two houses, and León lived there in the house behind our house for most of his life. He never married so after he died five years ago, we rented it out. Sandra was our first and only tenant, and lived there these five years. We became friends because she was a very good gardener, you can see how beautiful are the trees and bushes and flowers. And she taught my son José to boogie-board, and she taught us English. So we were friends. She was paying a small rent for some time, and then all the property around here became very valuable." She hesitated, then went on. "I am telling you part of this story too, my father's words and my own. We have three sons and so we never imagined that they would be able to go to the good schools and the university, but then, when all the land here in Sayulita became so rich we began thinking that our boys would leave here and make another life for themselves, instead of to be fishermen. But we wished for Sandra to stay here as long as she wanted, and so when she came to us with a proposal to buy the house and land we were happy to think about it. It turned out that she did not have the money to buy it, but she had found some partners who wished to finance it for her. They wanted to take the property and tear down the house and all the trees and make a big project, and a lot of money, but we did not wish to make Sandra leave, nor did we want a big project there, and we will not need this money for many years, because our boys are still young, so we made a deal with them that we would sell them the house and lot for a good price, but only with the condition that Sandra is able to stay there for as long as she wants up to ten years. We did not want to sell the place to any other person. This is what Sandra asked for, ten years, and so we did it. In ten years, we told them, we will need all the money, and you can do your project. They said that was good and in the meanwhile they paid us a down payment of fifty thousand dollars, which was very good as Pancho and my father could buy a new boat, and we have a nice car now, and next week a washer and dryer are coming from Puerto Vallarta so I will not be doing laundry this way any more, but the rest of the money—two hundred thousand dollars US—they were going to pay in ten years when Sandra could leave. And also the deal was that she had the right to buy the place at that price at that time, right of first refusal, they called it, if she wanted to stay longer. They seemed fine with this. I think they thought that Sandra would want to leave Sayulita by then, maybe she told them that, I do not know, but we knew that she wanted to stay here. And that she might even be able to buy it herself. So we took this chance, thinking that even if she left in ten years that we would be willing then to let them build their big project, because we can use the money to send the children to university. And maybe by then there will be so many noisy gringos in Sayulita that we will not care about living here." Her eyes filled with tears. "But then she died in the surfing contest—"

"Her rights to the place go to her family, yes?"

"No, they go to the partners. That was part of it too, you see. We never imagined her dying. We hardly even talked about this part of the contract. She was only twenty-seven years old. And now—"

Her husband finally spoke, in heavily accented English. "That *cabrón* Ruben Dario and his American partners plan to rip all the trees out and tear the house down and make some big ugly apartments over there, and sell them all. They are planning to start this building sometime in the summer. We get a lot of money that we don't need and they are going to ruin that land forever. I have lived here always and I have seen what this development brings. Our street will never be the same."

"Well Lucy, I guess we've got our motive," Mary said, her voice tinged with sadness as they trudged back down the road a few moments later. "And I've got some more great footage."

"Really. That old guy was so soulful—and true. What a sad story," Lucy said. "Sandra and her friends there had a wonderful plan, and then, conveniently enough for these stinking developers, she dies. You'd think they'd planned it that way, huh? Well, all I can say is the plot is certainly thickening. Into tragedy. But how are we ever going to be able to prove anything? How can we nail these guys?"

"I think you should get that Tweed character on this. I bet there's an email trail. These days there's always an email trail."

Back at the Internet café, Lucy logged on and discovered that Slope Tweed had sent her an email with a link to his Web site, seedytweedy.com. She went there and had a look. The site offered Internet services, no details beyond that. There was a photo of Tweed on the street in the East Village. He looked like Homer Simpson in black hipster clothes. Lucy sent him an email: *Hi Slope. Lucy R here. Saw your site. Mickey says you can find things out. The company is Sayulita Development Company, Web site Sayulitaforsale.com. Any email from anyone there, especially a guy called Ruben Dario but also Wally Townsend, to someone called Judy Leggett, JudyLegs @Yoohoo.com; any email between any of them and SanDar @mns.com. If you could cover the last month that would be great. Do your best. We think these people are guilty of murder. Also PLEASE do what you have to do to make this email completely go away at both ends. Thanks Lucy Ripken.*

9

A Showdown and a Letdown

There were plenty of threads to untangle, but chief among them, to Lucy's thinking, was the mysterious role of Judy Leggett. What was her stake in this deal? Lucy hoped the email trail, should Slope Tweed come up with one, might resolve that, but meanwhile she thought she'd drop in on Bobby's house and have a look around. With Mary's digital mini-cam in one hand, she pedaled her fat-tire bike up the hard-packed low-tide beach, shooting filler material. Now that the *X Dames* had folded up its tents and faded into the background, dead surf-chick included, Sayulita life had returned to its eccentric norm: as she swooped up the beach, she grabbed footage of castle-building kids, tussling dogs, soccer-playing Mexican teenagers, beer-swilling California surfer-dudes, joint-toking Euro-hipsters, and margarita-sipping high-rent daytrippers from Puerto Vallarta, vamping on rented lounge chairs. She taped the town's resident surfing dog—a small black-and-white mongrel, he rode the nose while his tattooed owner-man carved up a dinky little wave on his longboard—as she passed the point. North of the point the crowd thinned, and she surreptitiously captured pairs of well-groomed *Norteamericanos* power-walking the sand, their well-groomed lapdogs marching in leashed lockstep. When she reached the house of the big fat moon she parked the bike by the beach steps, went up, and approached cautiously, still shooting.

When she got closer, she heard cries and moans, not of pain but of pleasure; sexual pleasure. She stopped, uncertain, and then heard clear as day, Bobby Schamberg saying, "Awesome, baby. Keep it going. Oh, yeah." This definitely required a closer look. She crept up to the window, minicam ready, and peered into a large bedroom. On the king-sized bed in the middle of the room, beneath a ceiling mirror, *El Pantero* the surfing champion lay on his back, naked and fully aroused, fondling himself while he waited for the girls to warm up. Next to him on the bed, naked, intertwined and writhing, Henrietta and Judy worked on each other. They both had gone Brazilian down below, Lucy could not help but notice. Bobby stood a few feet away from the bedside, also naked and aroused, shooting the scene with a video camera. Lucy shot thirty long seconds of footage, then ducked down and scurried away. That clip would probably not make it into the movie. Or maybe it would, if they ended up in the edgier precincts of cable, where hard-ons went uncensored, tits and ass were everywhere, and people talked that pottymouth talk and called it hard-boiled dialogue. Who knew?

What Lucy did know was that she was dealing with a number of people of dubious moral character. But then, she'd already known that. Or maybe she was turning prude. In any case, her reaction to what she'd just seen was not to get aroused, irritated, amused, or intrigued. She felt just slightly disgusted.

That's what she told Marcia and Terry when she showed it to them on a computer a bit later in the afternoon, when they met back at the hotel. "God, I can't believe I slept with that guy," Marcia said after watching.

"Hey, you were drunk, kid," Lucy said.

"Yeah, but I'm not stupid. I was just—"

"He's a total stud, you guys," said Terry. "There's no denying that. I mean look at him. You're a horny twenty-three-year-old girl and that guy has a body to die for. With some serious lumber included. So save the guilt for a more worthy occasion. In any case I'm more interested in that shadowy other body—right there—myself," she said, freezing the computer screen in the midst of the little orgy as they replayed it. "Look at that." She pointed. There was a man standing in a doorway, partially visible, whom Lucy hadn't noticed when she'd poked her camera in the window or even when they watched it the first time. She'd been—distracted. They blew the frame up and manipulated it for a moment, until they were sure: none other than Ruben Dario, enjoying the show.

"Are you sure Bobby's not in on this whole scheme?" Lucy said to Terry. "I mean, he's really in the thick of it, Ter."

"He told me this morning he'd talked Henrietta and Judy into doing a movie with that Panther guy," she said. "I remain convinced he's not in on the 'plot,' whatever it is. Aside from everything else, he doesn't need the money. I guess I never told you, but I suspect Bobby's true aspiration is to become a porn mogul. He's been shooting and collecting homemade triple-X footage like this for years."

"That is so gross," said Marcia. "I knew this one girl who ended up, you know, out in the Valley doing hardcore. It was so weird, she showed up at this party, the last time I saw her, and she was acting like a real movie star. She calls herself Sheryl Deep, and my friend who's into porn told me every movie she was ever in her big scene, what they call the money shot, was the one where the guy, or guys, blasted her in the face with their orgasms. It was ugly."

"Porn ain't pretty, that's for sure," said Lucy. "And this whole scene is definitely getting seriously sleazy, isn't it? We verge on *Triple X Dames* here." She stopped. "But I still don't get why Judy stuck her neck out by giving the drugs to Sandra, except maybe she thought her true love Henrietta might win the contest if Sandra wasn't able to compete."

"But everybody knew Henrietta couldn't surf as well as half the other girls out there, Luce," said Terry. "There was no way she was going to win unless the bitch poisoned everybody in the contest."

"You're right. So I guess we'd better hope that Mr. Slope's got something for us. Shall we head down to the café for a look?"

They did, and there was an email from Slope: *Hey Lucy, getting this done was way easy for the seedytweedy. As was making your email disappear into the void, so no worries there. It would take a far smarter crew than this bunch to track me down. These people all had their passwords sitting right out there practically in the open for me to grab. They're either stupid or lazy or both. But there's a lot of junk. I don't know what you're looking for so I didn't dare edit. It's in six attachments. Each one covers a week's worth of correspondence between the names you gave me, sorted by date. Good luck, kick butt, hope to meet you sometime since Mickey says you're way past cool. El Slopo Mexicano.*

They downloaded the attachments and split them up between the two laptops and the desktop in the café. Marcia stayed at the desktop with her two weeks' worth, while Lucy and Terry headed back to the hotel to work through the other month of mail.

Four hours later, bleary-eyed but verging on triumphant, they stopped, reconnoitered, and made a few calls. First, Terry called Bobby and told him to plan a meeting at his house, next morning, nine a.m., and to get everybody there including Dario, Townsend, Judy, and Henrietta. Then Lucy called Dario's office to personally deliver the same message. Violeta claimed he was out of town again. Lucy said, "Fine, but let him know that I know everything about the deal with the Pastor and Caselin families, and I know a certain Dr. Cardozo in Bucerias, and . . . "

"Señorita Ripken," Dario interrupted. "I just walked into the office and Violeta tells me you are on the phone for me. Can I help you with something?" She'd heard him breathing the whole time, listening and breathing, just like when he'd been watching them shoot their sex movie up at Bobby's house.

"Tomorrow. Nine a.m. Bobby's house. You know, where you were watching Bobby make a movie this afternoon. Hope you got off good. You can help by being there, and bring your partner." She hung up.

"Damn, you're a fierce one, Luce," Terry said.

"I think we'd better watch out for that guy," Lucy said. "He knows we know stuff."

"Well, you might say you're pushing a few of his buttons, Lucy," Marcia said.

"And that's why we love you, Luce," said Terry dryly. "Meanwhile, let's get Mary in here to document our email finds. These are major leads."

They tracked Mary down by calling around town, and she showed up soon thereafter. They shot several scenes with each of the women making incriminating email finds. This was reality staged, yes, but the emails weren't. They were solid bits of cyber-info, undeniable truths even if obtained by dubious means.

After a run to the liquor store for a bottle of Sauza and a stop at El Juicy to print out a couple dozen pages of emails, the women spent the evening knocking back shooters while weaving their lovely web of accusations. They were done just short of midnight.

Unwilling to go back to Bobby's house at this point in the drama, Mary spent the night on Lucy's sofa, leaving her matching bed boys on their own for the night. "They'll be OK by themselves," she said. "I think they like screwing each other more than they like doing me." She sighed. "But at least they don't ask me to make movies of it."

"They've been invisible all week, Mary," Lucy said. "They're like—pet dogs."

"Exactly," Mary said. "A fine pair of puppies."

After breakfast the four of them headed up to Bobby's, accompanied by Hector Valdez and his camera. Mary also had hers, so they could get a couple of different camera angles on what they hoped would be the climactic confrontational scene. The Big Bust. Bring Down the House.

The usual fleet of SUVs had parked in the driveway. They went in the open front door and found them all sitting in the living room: Bobby Schamberg, Judy Leggett, Ruben Dario, Henrietta Walton, and Wally Townsend. Violeta was there too, in her sexy secretary outfit, with a notepad and a pen, ready to take dictation. The other surfer-girls and the surf-stud, uninvited, were not on the scene. Mary's boys, their "work" done, had gone home on an early flight. "Hi girls," said Bobby. "How are you today?"

Terry went to a wall switch and turned all the lights on high. "We're good, Bobby," she said. "I hope you're well, after your strenuous—workout—yesterday afternoon."

He smirked. "God, do you guys like, have to know about everything?"

"Not only know it, Bobby, my man," Terry said. "We have to document it."

"Please," Dario cut in impatiently. "I have many things to do today. Can you kindly make me to understand why we are here?"

"Well," said Lucy, a little nervous now that they had set the stage, and the cameras were rolling. "Nice of you all to show up on time."

"Now as you know," she went on, "Teresa MacDonald and I, *X Dames* writers, have had our doubts about the stated cause of Sandra Darwin's death in the surfing contest the other day. These doubts were raised by a number of facts, the central one being that someone drugged me that morning—and though we never had a chance to prove it we believe that the drugs I ingested were in coffee that Sandra also drank." She was being too formal, she decided. Too stiff. This was performance! The camera was on her. Lighten up, Luce. "So, gang, here's what we did. We found out about Sandra's real estate deal, and her partners. We found out where she lived, and how she bought the house. We found out—"

"Wait a second, Lucy," Terry interrupted, on cue. "You're getting ahead of yourself here. All in good time." She held up a sheaf of papers. "Although we were able to dig this stuff up only after we'd looked into the real estate deal, these emails turned out to be quite revealing about what happened before the surfing contest was even set up.

"What we have here, amigos, is a number of emails sent between Ruben Dario's office and Judy Leggett, and even a few involving you, Señor Townsend, and you, Henrietta. They date back a couple of months, to a period just prior to the decision by Judy and Bobby to stage the surfing contest in Sayulita, and date forward until last week. It seems that Judy knew Ruben Dario from previous surfing trips—and also they both knew Sandra, and knew exactly her living circumstances. You, Ruben Dario, knew Sandra even better than most, for in spite of having a wife and three children living in Santa Barbara, California, you were involved in an affair with Sandra. And following from that information and several of the emails we discovered, it looks to us as if the point of having the contest here, in Sayulita, was to set up a situation that you—Judy and Ruben—might use to your advantage—as in, somehow getting Sandra to buy the Caselins' property, where she had been living for several years, since as you very well knew she had become friendly with her landlords. You knew they would never sell that property to you, because they did not want that land developed or Sandra's pretty little house torn down. So the idea was to get her to buy it and then get her rights to it. This was your idea, Ruben, so you were quite happy, even eager, to lend Sandra the down payment of fifty grand, seemingly no strings attached.

"Once Bobby signed on to the Sayulita location for the *X Dames* show, on Judy's advice, it became a matter of coming up with a plan to get hold of the property, and the easiest and most obvious way to do this, you decided, was to somehow get rid of Sandra. I know you considered bribing her—buying her out for a fat chunk of money—but you were not convinced she would take your money to betray her friends, the Pastors and Caselins. Then you lucked out when Judy's wavetracker reported a major swell was going to show up this week, raising the possibility of a surfing accident, say, during the contest, when the women competitors would be expected to take chances in the waves, to score more points. Of course Judy knew Doctor Cardozo, she'd been down here a few times on surfing trips, so she knew she'd be able to get as much dope as she needed, OxyContin for herself, and Seconal for whatever other purposes.

"Henrietta, aside from bad taste in lovers and friends, your only problem is that you knew what Judy planned to do to Sandra, so you're guilty of accessory. You figured, I guess, that it might give you an actual shot at winning the contest. Townsend, you're just a greedy fuck with no heart, happy to come along for the ride and collect your commissions. Bobby, you're the horndog supreme, incapable of thinking with anything but your dick. We find it hard to believe that you weren't aware of any of this, but I don't think you were. The rest of you, well, we have evidence in writing, right here, of a fairly solid case for conspiracy to commit murder, since you are all on the deed to Sandra's property as partners or investors. With Ruben as *prestanombre*—we know that Sandra's neighborhood has not yet been regularized so that there was no bank trust involved—you were all set to move forward, turning the fifty grand you paid the Pastor and Caselin family into what, five, six, seven million dollars?" She stopped.

"There's no way—I dump all my email every week," Judy said. "You're just making this shit up."

"You guys are utterly stupid when it comes to email. Anyone with half a brain knows once you write and send an email it remains in your computer, somewhere, unless you proactively delete it. It was a simple matter to dig them all out. And here they are," Terry said, waving her stacks of paper. "Your names, email names, your scheme to make sure the contest was down here, your plan to approach Sandra with your falsely generous offer to help her buy her house, the deal to get the drugs and get some into Sandra's body on the day of the contest, all of it is right here, on paper."

"And now let's go to the video," Lucy said. They'd loaded all the footage onto one DVD, and now she slid it into the player so it would run on the big screen. "By the way, people," she said, "we have two more copies stashed elsewhere, so don't even think about trying to mess with this DVD. You'll be wasting your time." It began with the unedited footage from the breakfast, with Lucy describing the business about the dope in the coffee. Then they cut to contest footage interspersed with a series of stills Lucy had shot from the water, including several that showed Sandra collapsing on her board just before her deadly wipeout. Then they moved to the scene in Bucerias, tracking down Doctor Cardozo, and Teresa's description of what happened in the office. From here the story shifted to the real estate office, and from there to the scene at Sandra's house and the house behind it, where Mariela and her father and husband had their say. Finally, just for fun, they ended with thirty seconds of pornography that Lucy had shot the day before.

"Christ, why is that in there?" Bobby said. "You don't have to—"

"Bobby, don't forget this is going to be a movie of the week," Terry said. "That part will go away before it hits the little screen. But we thought it would be amusing."

"You can't be serious," Dario said with a sneer. "You can't make this into a movie!"

"Yes, we can, and we can also take it to the police, which we intend to do this very day," Lucy said.

"Señoritas," Dario announced, his tone turning supercilious as he rose to his feet. "You must wait a minute before you begin speaking about the police. Now I personally do not care what you want to show on television up in the United States, except that I hope it has a good audience because I have invested some money in this project. But I will tell you this. One, I don't know if you are familiar with Mexican laws about Internet privacy, but you have violated many of them. Therefore everything that you claim you have in those papers there is worthless as evidence, if that is what you think to use it for. Two, there is nothing in that video footage that incriminates anybody. The breakfast tells me nothing. The surfing footage shows somebody falling down. The business with the doctor, Señorita MacDonald here can make this up, and even if it is true, there is no reason that Judy Leggett, who has a documented history of back pain due to many surfing accidents, would not be legally able to obtain these prescriptions. I do not have anything to say about the Caselins and Pastors except that they are angry that they did not charge a higher price for their property, and now they want to blame me and my partners because we will be making so much more money. And finally," he said, "do you know the name of the district superintendent of the Mexican Federal Police? He is in Tepic, and he is the man who would be responsible for prosecuting this case, should you actually choose to drag your ridiculous pile of evidence up there and give it to him. At which time he might decide to prosecute you, ladies, because you have stolen private email.

"I'm sure you do not know him, or his name. But you see I do, because his name is Arturo Augustino Dario, and he is my younger brother." He stopped. The room fell silent for several long seconds.

"Shit," said Marcia.

Lucy and Teresa exchanged looks. Without saying a word they gathered the papers and the DVD and headed towards the door. Marcia followed them. Mary and Hector continued filming as they too moved towards the door. There, they all stopped. "See you in court," Lucy said, but her tone was defeated. Hector lingered in the doorway, shooting reactions. Mary followed the women across the driveway.

Hector's last shot from that sequence was one of Bobby, who muttered, "Good job, amigo," then raised his voice to announce, Donald Trump–style, "Hector Valdez, you're fired!" before slamming the door in his face.

Mary's last shot was Lucy and Terry in conversation.

Lucy: "We're screwed, aren't we? There's no way we can go after them, is there?"

Terry, shaking her head: "I don't think so. I mean I don't know if he knows what he's talking about regarding Internet privacy. But our case is primarily circumstantial any way you cut it, and if his brother is in charge of the local cops, you know he won't touch it." She brightened marginally. "But if Bobby will let us weave it in with the surfing contest, you know it'll make a great piece of TV, Luce. We'll call it *X Dames: Guilty As Not Charged.*"

10

Back in the Land of Money

The four women flew back to LA later the same day, up-
graded to first class courtesy of Bobby Schamberg. They
were uniformly depressed by their lost cause, but they also
felt rich: Lucy and Teresa surprised to find themselves on
the $2,500-a-week payroll for another week at least, Marcia
holding a Schamberg Productions *X Dames* Weekly Winner
check for twenty-five grand, Mary on contract and off to
Chile as soon as they got the first episode wrapped and in
the can. Bobby had instructed Mary to take all the footage
they had and turn it into a ninety-minute movie. He said
take no prisoners.

"So tell me, Marcia," Lucy said not long before they
were due to land at LAX, "What were you and your sister
up to the night before we left last week?"

"Up to? What are you talking about?"

"Come on, kid. I had to blow a horn in your ear to wake
you up. You had a pair of guys in your apartment who

looked like major lunatics. You had this weird chemistry set on your counter. You passed out on the plane. Your—"

"All right, all right," she said. "We were trying this shit my friend Jack—he was the major lunatic in my bed, and by the way he's gay so we don't even have a sexual relationship. Anyways he and his friend Theo smuggled this stuff back from the jungle in South America. It's called yage, you snort it and it feels like the back of your head's getting blown off, then you have this awesome visual and physical rush that lasts about half an hour, it's like a total universal revelation, and then it knocks you on your ass for ten hours. But if you don't cook and mix it right it's insanely toxic."

"Yage?" said Teresa. "Sounds like a mindfuck to me."

"It was that and more," Marcia said. "The last thing I remember seeing before I passed out was my dad, and he had turned into this giant worm."

"I can see that," Lucy said, then quickly added, "Just kidding," but Marcia laughed.

"I know, I know, he's kind of a sleaze," she said. "But he's all right, really. He's just had it too easy all his life, and then when he started getting old and realized he had gotten exactly nowhere and done pretty much nothing, he dumped my mom and got himself a candy girl. Someone who would be impressed by his bullshit and his bad art, unlike my mom and sister and me. That's why he looked like a worm to me."

"Well, now you can go to art school without hitting on him."

"I know. I'm thinking of moving to New York, Lucy," she announced. "To go to Pratt."

"It's not in Manhattan you know," Lucy said. "It's in the depths of Brooklyn."

"Yeah, I know," Marcia replied. "But I couldn't afford Manhattan anyways. Plus I can get to the waves on Long Island easier from Brooklyn."

"You're right about that," Lucy said. "With tuition and all, that twenty-five grand'll buy you a couple of months in Manhattan if you're cheap. And I hear the Hamptons and the whole south shore get really good in hurricane season. They say even Coney Island's rideable, and you can get there on the D train. But hey, I'll be in the same leaky boat if I can't get my loft back. I'm just a freelancer, kiddo, and I won't be working this *X Dames* deal much longer, I'm afraid."

"I can't believe no one knows who moved into your place," Mary said. "That's so bizarre."

"Actually I suspect the landlord knows exactly who's in there," Lucy said. "I'd be willing to bet he hired someone on the sly to do this, and even if he isn't behind it, if he's already met this woman, whoever she is, I'm going to have a hell of a time getting the place back because I'm sure he'll cut some kind of deal with her, jack the rent up and give her the lease he never gave me. This guy is really a pain. I've been in court with him pretty much ever since I moved in. But I've got my boyfriend working on getting this mystery impostor out of there, and he's pretty good at stuff like that." Except that he was not in New York working on anything. He was in Florida rooting around in the mud after buried treasure.

As soon as they landed she turned on her cell phone and discovered that Harold had called three times that very day. She checked the messages. "Hey Luce tried to reach you at the hotel but you were checked out. What's up? I've got news." "Luce, call me when you get this." "Where the hell are you, Lucy?"

She called from the plane and left him a voicemail. "Harry, I just got back. I'm here in LA. Lots of news. Call my cell."

He called while they waited for the baggage. "Hey Luce, how are you? How come you're back so soon?"

"I'm fine, treasure man. I mean considering that one of the surfer girls got murdered and I know it but can't prove it. But enough about me. How'd it go?"

"Murdered! What the hell are you talking about, Lucy? You got yourself into another situation, didn't you, you crazy dame!"

"Kind of. Officially this woman drowned, but there were drugs involved. Look, it's a complicated tale. I'll tell you the whole damn story when I see you. But right now I'm fine and I want to know how your deal went."

"It went—strangely."

"Strangely? What does that mean? Did you find your million, Harry?"

"No, I mean not exactly, but—"

"But what. Stop beating around the bush, Ipswich. What happened?"

"How come you're back so soon? I thought you were going to be down there for a couple of weeks."

"Harry, come on, you're playing with me. Our bags are coming down the belt and I gotta run."

"OK. Here's my story: me and my crew—Clarence and Harvey, the two Jamaican dudes I told you about—spent like five hours every night digging, and then shoring up the stinking mud with these wooden pallets we kept stealing from the back end of the store above us. The whole operation was an insane and stupid idea, I told myself every five minutes every night, as I was wallowing through the mud wondering if an alligator might decide to move into our burrow and eat one of us for dinner. I should have listened to you. And then eventually we got to where the money was supposed to be according to my calculations. And it wasn't there."

"So you didn't find it. Well what did I tell you, Harry? Didn't I—"

"At that point I should have bailed, but like I said to Clarence and Harvey, I know these guys weren't bullshitting me. I just know it. Plus I was already into this for around two thousand bucks so I wasn't quite ready to give up. So they're like OK, mon, we not have to stop now, which way you want to dig further? They were each making a hundred and fifty dollars a day off me so why would they want to quit? So I closed my eyes and waved my arm around and then, since I had no clue which way to go, I just pointed and said, there. So we all went at it again, did another five feet, and there it was, lo and behold, a black plastic bag."

"So you found it?! You found the million dollars? Harry, I'm—"

"Not exactly. See, the money was actually in five separate smaller bags inside the one big bag. And unfortunately the drug-dealing dolts didn't seal them very well, so—" he stopped. "Four of the seals had been breached and the money had rotted away or been eaten by bugs, worms, whatever. It was all confetti and dirt. But," he stopped again, and waited, for dramatic emphasis.

"But what, Harry—that one's mine," she said to Marcia, pointing at a suitcase. "Could you grab it? Thanks."

"So I didn't get a million bucks but we did get the one bag that didn't leak—and it had two hundred grand in twenties in it."

"You got two hundred thousand dollars? Harry, that is amazing. Terry, he found the money!"

"The doper's buried million? I don't—"

"Most of it was rotten but he got two hundred thousand. Jesus, Harold, that is so amazing. I can't—"

"Actually I only have one-fifty because I gave Clarence and Harvey twenty-five thousand each."

"Is that what you agreed on?"

"No, I had told them 10 percent but when we actually got the money, it seemed like the right thing to do."

"Cool, Harry. Generosity is always cool."

"Yeah. And a hundred fifty grand ain't bad for a week's work, is it?"

"No it isn't, amigo. But it won't be enough to buy a loft if I can't get back into mine, will it?"

"God, that's right! Did you figure out who's in there, Luce?"

"I was hoping you were on the case, rich guy."

"I'm flying back day after tomorrow. I gotta wrap up some other business."

"I'll probably be out of here tomorrow myself. We've got some stuff to take care of, and I have to decide if I want to go to Chile to work on the show again—I'm feeling a little uneasy after what happened in Sayulita, to say the least—but first things first, and I really need to get back there and see about my loft."

"You do indeed, or Lascovich will be all over it. If he isn't already."

"He's been out of town I heard but I think he was due back today."

"You'd better get a move on, Luce. Well, listen, I gotta talk to this guy about alligators for my article. A hundred and a half is pretty fat but it ain't enough to retire on. I'll see you in a couple of days."

"Sounds good Harry. Love you."

"Love you, Luce. Hey, listen, I'll call my neighbor Antonio downstairs and tell him to let you into my place if you get there before me and the loft situation is still dicey. He's in 3C."

"Cool, Harry. Tell him elevenish tomorrow night. See you soon." She shut the phone. "Teresa, Harry found his money! He actually found two hundred thousand dollars buried under a Wal-Mart in the middle of a swamp in Florida!"

"Wow!" said Teresa. "That is amazing. We're all getting rich."

"What are you guys talking about?" Mary said.

"Yeah, what's this money story?" Marcia chimed in.

Lucy told the story of Harry's found dope money en route from LAX to Venice in Mary's black Lexus SUV. As she dropped off Teresa, and then Lucy and Marcia, Mary said she'd have a rough cut of *X Dames* episode one ready to show them the next morning, rushed because she was heading down to Chile to start shooting the snowboarding episode in two days. She also said, just before driving off, that she hoped they'd stay on the show in spite of what she called "Bobby's bad karma."

Lucy fetched Claud from Marcia's and walked him over to Teresa's place. They'd planned to hit the beach together to watch the sun go down. The door of Teresa's bungalow was open when Lucy got there. She went up and called in. "Hey Ter."

"I'm quitting," Teresa said, as Lucy walked in.

"Quitting what?" Lucy said.

"The stupid *X Dames*, Luce." She looked slightly stunned but immensely happy as she waved a letter of some sort at Lucy. "Pardon my goof-ball grin, Lucy, but I am in a state of simultaneous grace and shock. Luce, I got a McClellan."

"A McClellan? That's great I think, but what are you talking about? What's a McClellan?"

"The McClellan Fund. They give these grants in all kinds of different fields. I got one for art criticism. I don't even know who nominated me. It was probably Paxton, but they're not allowed to tell me. In any case they're going to pay me fifty thousand a year for the next five years. I can finish my book and do another one without even having to hustle. I am so made I can't even believe it."

"Jesus, Terry, that is phenomenal! Congratulations. God, is it totally payday or what?" They hugged. "That's fantastic! God damn! Plus you just made my decision way easier, kiddo."

"What decision is that, Luce?"

"Terry, you know the only reason I was even considering going on with this *X Dames* fiasco was you. The vibe was kind of ugly already and with what happened to Sandra I can't see working anywhere near that Judy, or Dario, again. I can't believe they'll even let Bobby keep us on if we don't quit. And I'd much rather quit than get fired, know what I mean? So: if you're off the show then I'm off too, so fast Bobby's not even gonna remember my name."

"Ha," said Terry triumphantly. "Let's let him pay us another week's salary, then we bail. Payday should be tomorrow."

"Sounds good. So when do you get the free money?"

"It says the first payment will be in September, twenty-five grand, then twenty-five more every six months for five years. And they pay the taxes."

"Amazing. I guess this calls for a celebration, Teresa MacDonald. What's the most expensive restaurant in LA these days?"

"I don't know but I bet Mary does. Let's call her. And get Marcia, too. We'll have a little reunion."

Mary was too busy editing and Marcia didn't want to go out that night so they moved the party to brunch the next day at Michael's Restaurant in Santa Monica.

Early the next morning the four of them watched Mary's rough cut of the premier/pilot of *The X Dames: Surf and Death in Sayulita*. Mary had done a wonderful job of putting the whole thing together visually, surf contest over-laid with murder investigation; she'd even done a tempo-rary voice-over narration. And at the end, when she asked, rhetorically, of the viewers, "And so who do you think is responsible for the death of Sandra Darwin?" it seemed quite clear, at least to this gang, whodunit.

"Bobby's gonna love it, Mary," said Lucy. "But what are you going to do about Judy Leggett and Ruben Dario? They look totally guilty."

"Nothing. Bobby said take no prisoners. This is the story we need to tell. If they can't live with it they'll have to bail on the show, but I think they both know that they stand to make a ton of money if the series flies. And I think it will. Surfer-babes, accusations of conspiracy to commit murder, and an exotic Mexican setting. What more could a network executive ask for? So I figure they'll just ride it out. They are a pair of evil, unethical assholes anyway, so why wouldn't they?"

Then a messenger showed up from Schamberg's office. He had money and letters for each of them. The checks were for $5,000 each, two weeks' pay, and the letters, signed with a Bobby stamp, regretfully informed them that their services were no longer needed as the show would be moving in a different direction commencing with episode two. "Damn," Lucy said. "I so wanted to quit first."

"Yeah, but now you don't ever even have to talk to that knucklehead again. Whereas I have at least another six hours of interviewing him about his daddy to look for-ward to. Hey, let's go spend some of his money!" Off they went to brunch. The four of them ate the best of everything off the menu and downed several bottles of shockingly expensive wine, running up a tab of nearly eight hundred dollars. Paying the bill gleefully, Terry said, "That was my entire income for the months of January and February of this year, girls."

Mary headed back to her house in Silverlake to work on the edit, while Lucy and her two compadres went back to Venice. She gave Claud his doggie downers and took him for a walk. Then she and Terry loaded all her stuff into the back of the little orange VW. It had been eight days since she arrived in LA. She told Marcia that she could stay with her in New York indefinitely if she did decide to go to Pratt and needed a place—assuming I have a place myself, Lucy added, and leave the yage in LA, please—and then Terry drove Lucy to the airport and the two women hugged and said their goodbyes. Lucy checked in her dog and her bags, and headed to the gate. She was due at LaGuardia at ten p.m. east coast time. She settled into her first-class seat and soon the wine caught up with her and she fell asleep, only to dream of falling out her loft window on the crest of a very large wave. An hour before landing, she woke up with a headache, worried. Back to reality. Real estate combat.

11

Manhattan Lullaby

In a cab en route from LaGuardia, Lucy called her own land line, and discovered, no surprise, that it had been disconnected without a forwarding number. She had the cabbie drive by the building and stop down the block. She looked up. The lights were on, the shades drawn. Could she see a silhouette moving up there, an evil, black, spiderlike shadow against the white shades she'd finally installed last year? She briefly considered hiking up the stairs and simply knocking, to see what would happen, but she knew what would happen: whoever the sly bitch was in there would not answer the door. She thought of going to Jane's and climbing up the fire escape and smashing her way in through a window, using an axe and the element of surprise, but somehow the very thought of such combat exhausted her. As did the idea of buying a gun somewhere and shooting out the lock. This was not a viable option.

Here she was back in Manhattan and fundamentally nothing made sense. She wanted to go home but someone else lived there, in her loft. Some anonymous person had stolen her home. Why did life in New York always have to be so difficult?

Instead she had the cabbie take her and her heap of suitcases and her groggy dog to the East Village, where she paid him an extra fifty dollars to carry her suitcases up to Harold's floor and put them outside Harold's door. She waited by the cab in the warm May air of New York, watching her stuff. There were fewer bad guys and more cops now but it was still nighttime in New York so you had to watch your stuff.

When the cabbie came down she went upstairs, banged on 3C, and collected a key from a guy named Antonio, who turned out to be Antonia, a gorgeous Puerto Rican drag queen who managed to let her know in the space of thirty seconds' interaction that he loved Harold madly and she was one lucky girl to have him.

"*Muchas gracias,*" Lucy said, and hiked down the hall and up the grungy stairs to Harold's place. There she found Claud, still a little woozy but oddly attentive, standing at Harry's door staring at the knob expectantly. Lucy stuck the key in the lock and after monkeying around a bit, she turned it, and pushed the door open.

Surprisingly, the room felt cosy, and candlelit, and smelled of—Harry! There he stood, in wine-red pajamas, with a frosted bottle of champagne in one hand, and two flutes in the other. He looked utterly ridiculous in the lounging jammies, but at the same time totally sexy. "Harry! Jesus, you're home!"

"Surprise, baby," he said. She ran to him, jumped up and wrapped her arms around his neck, and planted a wet kiss on his clean-shaven face. He put the champagne and glasses down and took her in his arms. The door slammed shut. "I finished and came home early, just for you."

"Wait, my stuff's out there," she moaned as he kissed her passionately.

"It can wait, baby," Harry murmured, all amorous intent. His hands worked on her body. She could feel herself giving it up, melting into his desire.

"Whoa, Harry, hold on a minute, lover boy," she said, pushing him off.

"OK, OK, Luce," he said, letting her loose, his hands lingering on her, tingling on her. He had such finely tuned fingers. They always knew where to go. Lucy felt dizzy, light, in love. "Let's get your stuff in here and have a glass of champagne and then—"

"I'm yours, baby," Lucy said, stroking her fingers down his chest, giving his pajama waistband a little tug. "So silky, Harry. Are these new?"

"I got roses, champagne, and pajamas on the way from the airport," he said. "Perrier Jouët. A little splurge." The red, red roses glowed in a vase on his little kitchen dining table. Candles flickered in the bedroom nook beyond. "Let me get the stuff." He got her suitcases and brought them all in, with the last one announcing, "My God, Luce, I forgot how heavy you travel sometimes," and then double-locked the door. By the time he turned around, Lucy had moved into the bedroom nook. He grabbed the champagne and glasses, and followed her in. And in his tiny East Village love grotto he got to watch Lucy as she slowly unbuttoned her little black sweater, and pulled her short black T-shirt over her head, and unsnapped her black jeans, and kicked off her shoes, and came to him, naked from the waist up, and took the glasses and the bottle from his hands. She put them down and took his graying head in her hands and brought his mouth to hers, and kissed him. And then moved him lower, to where he lingered over her breasts as she gave herself to him.

They fell on the bed, finished undressing, and then, when they were naked, and close—Lucy stopped short. "Harry," she said in her intimate voice, stroking him softly, making him hard. "Do you think I have—I mean, have you noticed that a lot of women are like, doing stuff to their pubic hair?"

"What are you talking about, Lucy?" Harry laughed, and touched her down there in just the right way.

"I'm talking about shaves, and trims, and styles, and . . ."

"God, that is so—I told you LA was the inferno, Luce. The inferno of bad taste, for one. You know what you're talking about? It's the porno industry migrating into the mainstream. Where else would you find people concerned about pubic hairstyles?"

"You have no idea, Harry, of some of the shit I saw this week," Lucy said, and then kissed him again, and pulled his body on top of hers. "I think I'm ready for you, money guy. How about we have some good old-fashioned sex?"

That they did, making love, drinking champagne for a while, making love again, and then, after Lucy told Harry an abbreviated story about what happened in LA and Sayulita, they slept intertwined in Harry's small double bed in his tiny sleeping nook in his itsy-bitsy walk-up. As blissed-out as Lucy felt, falling asleep in the arms of the man she loved pretty much all the time, the shadow of worry fell over her, for she knew, looking out Harry's one window onto the brick wall across the alley, that she could never live here with him. Not in this cramped, dingy little space. She knew that she could not live in New York if she couldn't get her loft back, with or without Harry. He'd said, murmuring off to sleep, that they'd figure something out, he was sure of it, but what that something was he did not say, and Lucy did not know.

After they made love again in the very early morning, Harold came up with a plan, not much of one, but it was a start. Good old-fashioned surveillance. After taking Claud for a dawn romp in Tompkins Square, they dropped him back at Harold's apartment, then speed-walked to SoHo in time to arrive at the Cuban coffee shop on the ground floor of the building catty-corner to Lucy's loft at seven a.m., when Ignacio opened. They set up shop at the table by the window, eating toast and slurping down sweet steamy Cuban-style *cafe con leche*. They waited and watched as Lucy's neighbors, one by one and two by two, emerged from the building in their daily routines. By nine everybody from all the floors except Lucy's had come out and headed off to their jobs; excepting Jane, a painter with a trust fund who worked at home. Jane, who'd made the mistake of letting the woman in, and yet was Lucy's only real friend in the building. The rest of them were partners in the assorted landlord-driven lawsuits they'd been fighting forever, but none of them were really friends. Only Jane, who finally came down at ten a.m. to get her mail. She stepped out onto the street just as Lascovich, the landlord, pulled up in his late-model ruby-red Chrysler, parked illegally in front of the fire hydrant, and emerged from his car, wife in tow. The wife went in the entry of the building next door, where Lascovich's business occupied the second floor. "Damn," said Lucy, her fourth cup of Café Cubano rattling in her hand. "Landlordovich is back. And all over Janey." The two of them were head to head, toe to toe, yammering at each other angrily. That went on for two minutes, then Lascovich jumped back in his car and drove off. "He's just going to park," Lucy said, dashing out. "I've got to talk to Jane." She stopped on the corner and shouted, "Jane, Janey, hey, over here." Jane looked up and around, and spotted her. She waved, waited for the light to change, and made her way over.

"Hey Lucy," she said. "You're back early." She looked downcast. "I guess because you're trying to get back into your place."

"Yeah," Lucy said. "How goes it?"

"God, Lucy, I am so sorry about what happened. I don't know what I was thinking. This woman was so convincing."

"Does Lascovich know she's up there?"

"Yes. God, it looks bad, Luce. I was just arguing with him about that. He's apparently given her a lease."

"A lease? How can he give her a lease? She's not even—"

"Unfortunately, possession is nine-tenths of the law, as our dear friend Jack Harshman likes to say, Lucy. When he's talking about the building. And at the moment she's got possession."

"Well who the hell is she?" asked Harold from the restaurant doorway, where he hung back, out of sight.

"God, I wish I knew. Maybe Lascovich planted her in there himself since he knew you were leaving. But I have no idea how she knew what she did about you, Lucy."

"It is strange, isn't it?"

"And Lascovich has changed all the entry door locks, and the elevator locks. He had to give us all keys, of course, but you're not going to be able to get in there with the keys you have. I'm pretty sure the new tenant also changed the locks on your door, because the locksmith was up on your floor for a while after he did the building doors."

"God damn, I can't believe this," Lucy said.

"There's Lascovich now," Harry said. Lascovich strutted down Broome Street, scowling at the world. "Maybe you should make yourself scarce, Luce." She ducked in, followed by Jane.

They sat at the table. "So what's the plan?" Jane said. "I can get you copies of the new street door keys, but that's not going to get you into your loft."

"This woman has been in there, what, almost a week, and you haven't seen her since the day she moved in?"

"I don't know what she's doing up there, Lucy, but I swear to God she has not come out since she went in. Not that I'm always there but I am there most of the time."

"Listen," said Harry. "We need to find out who she is. Lascovich doesn't know me so I'm going to go to him, act like I'm looking for a place to rent, and see if I can find anything out. Here's what I'm thinking." He laid out a plan. Jane went off to get keys made. Lucy put on her sunglasses and went out onto Broadway and headed south, looking for a heavy object. Harry crossed the street and went into the building next door to hers, to visit Lascovich in his office. She thought Harold's plan to be sketchy, since the results, most likely, would be nothing more than a name. But they needed to move fast, for the longer Lucy was out of the loft the more difficult it would be to get back in. Harold seemed to think this would serve as a starting point.

Ten minutes later she waited down the block, across the street, on the corner of Broadway and Grand. She'd found a fist-sized piece of brick at a construction site down Grand, and now she waited. Her cell phone rang, once. The signal. "Christ," she muttered, talking to herself. "This is such a bad idea." She did it anyway. She crossed Broadway on the green light, walked north, and then, when she reached her destination, she simultaneously stumbled and threw the brick as hard as she could at the glass-paneled entry door to the ground-floor landing of Lascovich's office. The panel shattered as Lucy fell carefully onto the sidewalk so as not to hurt herself. An alarm began blaring loudly inside the entryway.

"Are you all right?" a passing guy asked, stopping to help her to her feet. Crowds streamed past, a busy workday morning on Broadway, everybody intent on getting where they needed to go, right now.

"Yes, I'm fine, thanks," she said. "I guess there was a brick or something. I must have kicked it." She brushed dirt off her jeans.

"I'll say," he said, as people swarmed by, not noticing the mini-drama playing out. "You kicked it right through that door."

She heard them coming down the stairs. "Wow, that's something, huh?" she said, extricating herself from his helpful hands and strolling up the sidewalk. "Well, I've got to run—" She zipped across the street in a mini-mob of people just as Lascovich emerged onto the sidewalk in a rage, followed by his wife. The man who'd helped her up must have tried to explain, because Lascovich's eyes darted up the street after her a moment later, but by then she'd crossed Broadway in a knot of moving bodies and slipped back into the coffee shop, where Ignacio poured her another. She tapped on the counter twice, and then raised an eyebrow, and he quickly pulled a bottle of rum out from under the counter and hit her coffee cup with a shot. "Thanks, amigo," she said, taking a big gulp. "I needed that."

"No problem, Lucy," Ignacio said. She'd been drinking his coffee for five years, and every once in a while she needed a bump from the illegal bar under the counter. A liquor license was a pricey thing. He was happy to provide that occasional shot.

Harry came in five minutes later. "Mission accomplished. Good job with the brick, Luce. You totally took out the door."

"I did feel a certain satisfaction, watching that glass shatter. You get a name?"

"I got some photographs. Break out the laptop and let's have a look." While they set up and downloaded he went on: "That Lasko's really after you and your building mates. And he seems to think he's got something going. I asked about renting a place in his building and he said there was nothing available but he thought that maybe in the building next door that he also owns he would have something coming up soon. I asked at what rent, he said $3,000 a month and up."

"Jesus, I'm paying—"

"Six hundred. So now you know what the market will bear, Luce."

"No wonder he's after us."

"When the alarm sounded he and his lumpen missus went downstairs so I tore through his desk at high speed, and shot what looked interesting as quickly as I could. I think I got six pictures."

The first three were useless. The fourth was a commercial lease dated May 10, for five years, for a rent of $2,800 a month for the fifth floor premises at 486 Broadway, etc. Lessor Itzak Lascovich, lessee Sandra Green. "Sandra Green?" Lucy said. "The name kinda rings a bell, but—"

"What kind of bell?"

"I don't know, I guess it's just a sad coincidence. The woman who died in the surfing contest was also named Sandra."

"That's too bad—but it's really not that uncommon a name, Luce."

"I know, I know." She looked at him intently. "So now what, maestro?"

"I say we break the goddamned door down, Lucy."

"What about using the cops here, Harry? Maybe we should play this one straight."

"Lucy, do you want to get your loft back? If we do this through legal channels it could take months. Lascovich will be all over it. You'll be in a much better position if you're already in, with your documented history of living there."

"You're right, Harry. So—what do we do?"

"Call Jane. Tell her we need to get into her place. She owes you on this. We'll go up the fire escape from there, and I'll take out a window with a baseball bat if I have to."

"And what about Sandra Green?"

He gave her a look. "We'll do what we have to, Lucy."

Lucy called Jane, and they made the arrangements. By the time Jane came down to let them in, Lascovich's workers had cleaned up the shattered glass and stuck a plywood panel onto the door. He and his wife were back upstairs in their office.

They trooped up to Jane's place—the elevator remained unfixed—and went in. Her place was cluttered with paintings of dogs, for that's what she did. Painted dogs. She did lovely dog portraits for uptown ladies, and street drawings of mutts for downtown dudes. But her floor layout was much the same as Lucy's: at the far northwest corner, three steps rose to a door that led out onto a fire escape that hung off the north side of the building, overlooking Broome Street. A row of tall windows ran the length of that side of the building on each floor. Theoretically, they could go out on this level and go up one flight and from the fire escape somehow break into Lucy's place. Lucy had never installed alarms, the glass was ancient, the window-locks even more ancient. Harold had not a bat but a small crowbar, just in case the mysterious Sandra Green was there and had some muscle around. You never knew.

After checking to make sure Lascovich wasn't down on the corner where he could spot them, they went out and quietly ascended the fire escape from the fourth to the fifth floors. They found the shades up on all the windows, on both north and west sides. They looked in. No one moving. They tried the access door. Unlocked, weirdly enough. They opened it and went into Lucy's home.

"Oh no," she cried out, for they had walked into a place that had been utterly destroyed. Furniture broken, papers strewn, food thrown and smeared, shit everywhere, stench overwhelming, the scene was complete, hideous chaos—and there was no one to be seen. "Oh my God, Harry, she's ruined my house."

"What a fucking mess," he said. "Let's check the kitchen and bath. And keep it down, Lucy. She might—"

"You know she's gone, Harry. She did this and left," Lucy said.

"I wouldn't be so sure of that, Lucy Ripken," the woman said, emerging from the bathroom. She wore purple velvet bellbottoms, a skintight, ab-revealing stretchy T-shirt, and big tinted glasses; she wore her hair long and blonde, and had Claud the poodle on a very short leash. His head was muzzled. Harry made a move towards her but she tightened the leash and suddenly a knife appeared in her other hand. She held it to Claud's throat. He whimpered, scared. Harry stopped.

"Claud!" Lucy cried out. "What the—how did you—what are you doing with my dog?" she said.

"Well I don't know just yet," Sandra Green said. "It all depends, I guess, on what you two do next. Oh, by the way, I've certainly enjoyed staying here in your loft this past few days. It's quite a nice place." Eyes on them, she sat down, in the only unbroken chair in the kitchen. They were in the doorway between kitchen and main loft area, watching her. She held Claud tightly, with the knife close to his throat. Behind her, the refrigerator door hung open. All the dishes were smashed to scattered pieces, and the oven door was ripped off the oven.

"What the hell do you want, lady?" Harry asked. "For God's sake, he's just a dog. He's got nothing to do with . . . "

"Shut the fuck up, Ipswich," she snarled, and suddenly flicked the knife at Claud's ear, slicing it open.

"Jesus Christ," he said. "What the—"

"You're not Sandra Green," Lucy said, stunned. The snarl had done it. "Oh my God. You're . . . ?"

She took off the tinted glasses and smiled at them. "That's right, Lucy, you stupid bitch. It's me." With a browlift and augmentation mammoplasty and liposuction and facial implants and collagen injections and otoplasty. Everything was different except for her dark, nasty eyes, and the slightly cockeyed, kewpie-doll grin.

"Maria Verde," Lucy said. "I should have known."

"Goddamn," said Harold, he too as stunned as Lucy. Claud whimpered, his ear bleeding.

"What do I want?" Maria said maliciously. "I want you to know this, bitch. I wish I'd taken care of you in Jamaica, and I thought I'd taken care of you in Sayulita, but . . . "

"Sayulita? What are you talking about?"

"You think you're such a clever girl, don't you Lucy?" she said, and glanced down. "Oh dear, your little doggie is bleeding. Well," She stood. Claud's ear was streaming bright red blood; she'd hit some kind of vein. It didn't look serious, but it did look ugly. Lucy could feel Harold's tension. He was ready to go for her. Lucy restrained him with a hand on his arm. She did not want to lose her dog to this mad bitch.

"Can I please have my dog?" Lucy pleaded. "He's hurt."

"He's gonna be hurt a lot more if you try to come after me," she said. "Now get out of my way." They backed into the living room. She came towards them, Claud held tightly at her side, muzzled, bloody. "Here's the deal. I'm going out the door and out of here and if you come after me your dog is dead fucking meat. Understood?"

"Why should we . . . what guarantee do I have that you'll . . . "

"None, bitch. Would you like it if I stab him in the heart right now?" she said, pulling him tight and holding the knife to his chest as she dragged him towards the door.

"God, leave him alone. Please don't . . ." Lucy couldn't help herself. Tears streamed down her face. Harold was breathing hard, enraged.

"God damn you, Maria Verde," he said. "You are . . . "

"Save it, Ipswich, you stupid cop," she said. "I'm going so far away you'll never ever find me, not in Venezuela, not in Jamaica, and certainly not at the site of a certain snowboarding contest in Chile." She reached back and opened the door. Harold tensed, ready to attack again. As the door swung open she flicked the knife down, and slashed Claud's other ear. Lucy screamed as her dog yelped in pain. Maria dragged him out the door. "I'm telling you to stay in here for at least an hour. I've got a guy watching and he sees either of you come out this dog is dead." She smiled, and suddenly in spite of all the cosmetic surgery that she'd had, she looked exactly the same as she had on a Jamaican beach a couple of years earlier, pointing a gun at Lucy's heart. Ugly and insane.

She slipped out and slammed the door. After a beat, Harold went for it. "No Harry, you can't!" Lucy cried. "She'll . . . "

He stopped. "You're right. She'll slit his throat without thinking about it. Christ, what a . . . "

"Monster. My God. What do we do?"

"Wait an hour. Call the . . . call who? Who can we call, Lucy?" he said.

"Nobody, while she's got my dog," Lucy said.

"I just hope she doesn't . . ." he stopped.

"Kill him anyway," Lucy said. He hugged her as she cried. "God, how did she get into your place too? How did she get Claud?"

"That woman is nothing short of diabolical."

"How the hell did she know about all that *X Dames* stuff, Harry? Who is she, for God's sake?!"

They couldn't think of a single soul to call that could help, and Lucy did not want to tell the story to anyone until she found out the ending and so they occupied themselves with beginning the clean-up. Exactly one hour after she'd left, they were about to open the door to head out when Lucy's cell phone rang. "Lucy here."

"Is this . . . do you own a white dog. A big poodle?"

"Yes, I do," she said frantically. "Is he . . . "

"Hi. My name's Luciano. I found your dog chained to a fence in an alley off Great Jones Street a few minutes ago. He's all bloody but someone wrote this phone number on him so I called and . . . "

"He's all right?"

"Yes, he seems fine but he's all covered with blood from these weird slashes on his ears. I don't know what happened but . . . Oh, one other thing, there was a piece of paper taped to his collar that said on it, "You've got mail."

"You've got mail?"

"Yeah. That's it. Three words."

"Where are you?"

"At the Starbucks on Astor Place. The dog's still chained to the fence. I couldn't . . . sorry, but . . . "

"I'll be there in ten minutes. Stick around, I'll have something for you."

"Cool, lady." She hung up and handed the phone to Harold. "Call my vet, SoHo Animal Clinic on Prince, say we'll be there in half an hour. Call a guy who can cut chains and another who can make keys for this door. Once Lasko's gone for the day we'll get some made. I've gotta check my email."

Harold made the calls while Lucy set up her laptop and opened an email that had arrived a few moments past.

Dear Lucy

I hope this note finds you well. I must say, I did enjoy my stay in your lovely loft, and I hope that you appreciate just how lucky you are to have such a large and pretty home here in New York. Had you not shown up—the best-laid waves— oops, I mean plans—don't always work out exactly right—I might have enjoyed living here for a while.

As for me, I've been living "south of the border" since, well, since we last saw each other, but I do manage to get back home to the good old U.S.A. every now and then. By the way, did you not in all your years here learn about how you can get out of the building by going up on the roof and onto the building behind, on Crosby Street, and then into their stairwell and down to the street? They never lock their roof door, it seems . . . oh, but why would you need to know that?

I thought I was going to slit your dog's throat and leave him on the street out in front of your building, but he's got such sweet brown eyes, and I know from your stupid book about the Yucatán that he's just a poor little doggie who lost his real masters, so I decided to spare him. If you have gotten around to reading this email, then someone has no doubt called to let you know where I parked him. If it's been more than a day, well, I guess he'll be one hungry dog by the time you get to him.

Oh, by the way, I, too, know a good hacker, and so, well . . . about that money that Bobby Schamberg paid you, that

you put in your LA bank account? You can kiss it goodbye.
I've been having a lot of work done in Brazil, and I found
myself in need of a fresh infusion of funds.

I'll see you one of these years, Lucy Ripken, for I am not
done with you yet.

One last thing: In case you hadn't figured this out, I have
been working in the Industry for the last year or so, and in
the Industry I am known as Sophia Greenberg. Does this
come as a complete surprise? After Sayulita, I couldn't resist
the opportunity to pay homage to our late, great, surfer girl,
Sandra Darwin, and so this is farewell,

> *Love and Kisses,*
> *Your friend Maria "Sandra Green" Verde*

She printed it out and Harry read it while they hustled
up to get the dog and give this kid Luciano fifty bucks for his
trouble—he was there waiting when they got there, hanging
out behind a full and stinky alleyway Dumpster. Claud was
scared, dirty, and covered with crusted blood, but otherwise
OK. A guy with bolt cutters showed up a few minutes later
to cut the chain that had bound Claud to an iron railing.
They paid the bolt cutter guy and after a few minutes of pet-
ting and soothing, they took Claud to the vet. Once he was
in the vet's hands, they grabbed a couple of triple lattes and
headed back to the loft. By then, the day was nearly done
and Lascovich was gone. They met the keyman, a "specialist"
pal of Harry's, on the corner and he came up with them. After an hour he had the locks taken apart. An hour later he

had a new set of keys and locks in place. They paid him too much money and he left. As they cleaned up, they talked.

"Man, I had no idea she was that diabolical. Harry, we have got to—"

"To what? You know she's long gone, Luce. But at least you got your place back."

"Until Lascovich gets wind of us."

"Her lease ain't worth shit if she's not here, Lucy. Especially since the name she used is completely bogus." He frowned. "God, what is that woman's name, anyways?"

"Way back when, down Jamaica way, I heard she was once called Sophie Potts."

"Sophie Potts?"

"That's what Mickey told me."

"Well, that name isn't on any lease, that's for sure. There's no way that lease has any legal standing."

"Hope you're right, Harry. But I don't have one either, do I?"

"No but you've got a documented history of living here, right?"

"Shit," she said, and hurried back into the other room to look in her smashed-up desk. "It's gone."

"What?" He followed her.

"My documented history, Harry. I had a box of papers locked in this drawer."

"Jesus, Lucy, why didn't you take that stuff with you?"

"Harry," she said, and burst into tears, "don't blame me for—" she waved at the horrid mess that had been her home—"for this. Please, Harry."

He came to her, and held her. "I'm sorry, Lucy. That was lame of me." They hugged quietly for a moment, until she calmed down. She let go of him.

"Well, I'm going to keep cleaning up. But first, I need to make a few phone calls. I have got to put this thing together."

"What thing?"

"Harry, Maria Verde, or Sandra Sophie Greenberg Green or whatever she calls herself was working on the same TV show I was on. Don't you want to know how this happened?" Lucy flipped open her cell and speed-dialed an 800 number for a bank in LA. She punched in assorted codes, and then listened to her available balance, read to her by a computer: twenty-three dollars and forty-seven cents. She'd been robbed of nine thousand four hundred dollars. Next she called Teresa MacDonald.

"This is Terry."

"Ter, it's Luce in New York. I need to—"

"Hey Luce, long time no speak. Did you get—what happened with your loft thing? Did you find out—"

"I need to know one thing, Terry."

Teresa detected the intensity of her tone. "What's that, Luce?"

"Whose idea was it to hire me for the *X Dames*?"

"Mine. I mean Bobby's and mine. I think I suggested it, and—no, it was him. I remember now. He actually asked me to call you."

"Is he around?"

"Yeah, he came back last night. He called and said he didn't feel like he needed to be there on the snowboard shoot. Not enough sunshine or babes in bikinis I suspect."

"Do you have a number for him?"

"Bobby? Yeah, but why would you want to talk to Bobby? You're not—you didn't change your mind about working on the show, did you?"

"God no, of course not, Terry. It's just that I'm trying to figure out a really bizarre connection that I think he's part of."

"What's that?"

"The person who sneaked into my loft—and split before I could catch her, but meanwhile shredded the place and apparently stole all my money—was Sophie Greenberg."

"The producer? What are you talking about? She's down in Chile."

"She was. And is probably on her way back. But she's the one who—God, this is too weird. I met this woman a couple of years ago in Jamaica, and had a serious run-in with her. She almost shot me for breaking up a drug operation she had going. I think she changed her name to Sophie Greenberg somewhere along the line, and had some surgery done, and emerged, somehow, in Hollywood. Or Mexico, I don't know. But I'm trying to figure out how and why she hooked me into this deal."

Teresa was quiet for a moment. Then she said, "Well, if you guys really had some serious issues—you and Sophie that is—that would be the why of it. And I would say you just found a motive for what happened to you down in Sayulita as well. Lucy, all I can say is be careful. These are scary people. Here's Bobby's personal cell." She gave her the number. "I'll sign off since I'm sure you want to get on it. Keep me posted." They clicked off. Lucy punched in Bobby and he answered.

"Schamberg here."

"Hi Bobby, this is Lucy. Lucy Ripken, remember me?"

"Lucy! Remember you!? How could I forget you, baby? Hey, I'm sorry about the, ah, employment termination, but after what happened I didn't think you'd want to be working with my partners any more, and—"

"Forget about that, Bobby, its just sludge under the bridge at this point. But listen, I was wondering, I mean I know you said you read my book and I know that I came highly recommended by our mutual pal Teresa, but I really need to know who it was that first suggested that you hire me to work on the show."

"It was Terry, I'm sure—no, you know what, to tell the truth, I'm thinking back, and I remember Judy had a copy of your book before I even talked to Terry about it. And I think she said something about how you would be a good person to hire because you weren't a TV writer but you seemed tuned in to women's sports and also knew your way around Mexico. So yeah, I guess it was Judy. Why? What's up?"

"So how did you and Judy find Sophie Greenberg and Ruben Dario, your producer partners?"

"Judy knew Sophie from way back, she said. They met when Sophie was working as a writer and had interviewed her for a story on women's sports for one of those ladies' magazines. Then she'd been in and out of Latin America for a few years, and she'd made some great connections.

That's how we found Ruben. Hey, he had money to throw at us, what was I going to say? I mean to this day I'm not sure if you and Teresa got it right with your murder conspiracy thing, but it makes for a great subplot and I think we've got a hell of a show to open with as a result. Doncha think so?"

"I guess, Bobby. I'm glad it worked for you. Oh, just one other thing. Who does your books? You know, payroll and such, for Schamberg Productions?"

"That was part of Judy's gig."

"Right. That makes sense."

"What do you mean?"

"Nothing, nothing." She would have had Lucy's personal and financial information right at her fingertips. That money was gone for good.

"Cool." He paused. "So, ah, anything else?"

"Nope." She stopped.

"I'll see ya, Lucy."

"Sometime or other. Bye Bobby." She clicked shut, stood, took a deep breath, and then joined Harold, who'd already started cleaning up. Judy and Maria, old friends.

12

Loose Endings

Was this the end of the story? She couldn't help but ask herself two weeks later, after everything was cleaned up and painted and back to normal in her loft. By then, Harold had given Jack Harshman a five-thousand-dollar retainer to get Lascovich off her back. This had taken a bit of doing but eventually—in a rushed hearing called by Lascovich's lawyer, spying what he imagined was an opening that might lead to a successful tenant eviction—Lascovich did have to admit, squirming and snarling under oath, that yes, Lucy Ripken had lived in the space for over five years and yes, he had accepted rent from her for all of those years. Also there were copies of the checks written by Lucy to Lascovich, that Jack got from the bank. They kicked Lascovich's butt up and down the courtroom and that was that, until the next round.

And so home sweet home was home again, with a fresh set of locks. Money-flush Harold even bought Lucy an air conditioner on June 21st, the summer solstice, so the ninety-degree, 90 percent day outside magically went down to seventy degrees in her freshly painted, climate-controlled house.

They plunged into the sour depths of summer, which Lucy once upon a time had imagined, when she was rich and famous and working in the Industry a month or so back, would be spent in the balmier climes of Southern California, rather than stuck downtown in this torpor-producing, brain-slogging Manhattan heat; which she could not truly relax into ever, and even less so now, wondering where and when Maria Verde might strike again.

The woman had gotten under her skin. There was no way around it.

Lucy heard from Terry in July. The *X Dames* television premiere had been set for a late August Saturday night on the Outside Network. Definitely the dog days in TV land. The only thing working in their favor, Terry said, was that rumor had it, and rumor was everywhere in the Industry, that, in addition to the surfing contest and the murder investigation swirling around it on this reality show, there was supposedly some seriously cool hard-core triple-X footage of several very buff champion surfer girls, in the company of at least one male surfing champion, going at it in a very big bed. So speculation went, bubbling up from the depths of the Hollywood rumor swamp to surface in bits and pieces of stories in *Variety* and the choicer gossip columns on the left and right coasts. There in the doldrums of late summer they had a bit of a buzz on.

Sometimes a little buzz can go a long way.

On August 17th, four days before the show's premiere, Schamberg Productions announced that the *X Dames* episode one debut would be followed one week later by the second *X Dames* event, a snowboarding competition that had taken place in the Chilean Andes a week after the surfing contest.

The same night that announcement was made, and ran everywhere it needed to, a gardener called Max, who'd been working at Bobby Schamberg's Malibu house, was arrested and charged with his murder. Schamberg had been shot three times, in the head, chest, and groin, and died in a helicopter en route to St. John's Hospital in Santa Monica. Lucy heard it on *Entertainment Tonight*. Late that night she got a call from Teresa.

"Hey, it's me in LA."

"Hey Ter, how goes it?" The whole *X Dames* thing had cast a strange pall over their relationship. Nothing bad had really come between them, but they'd seen and been done some serious wrong, and had been unable to do anything about it. Things had shifted as a result. The Verde poison, seeping.

"Passably. I was inches away from completing Schamberg at long last when this miserable business with Bobby came down. So now I have to do another bit about his sad fate and tie it into the tragic arc of his father's life.

"But that's not why I called. I called to tell you Al DeLuca kicked the proverbial bucket this morning, lung cancer having had its way. And it's really too bad about the timing. He was going to have an opening of his pussy paintings, sure to stir a controversy and put the old goat back in the public eye, at the Cool-Ray Gallery next month. But now the show is postponed indefinitely and his death is overshadowed, to his eternal irritation no doubt, by the demise of our dear pal Bobby Schamberg."

"Poor Al. Poor Bobby. Bobby I knew about."

"So I figured. Been watching *ET* and its ilk way more than you should, right?"

"Yeah. It's utterly stupid but all the TV stuff seems—I don't know—like I've been there so I need to know."

"Trust me, you don't. But listen, I thought you might want to savor these little nuggets, which I picked up in what had to have been one of the coldest and most heartless voicemails I've ever gotten." She paused.

"What?" Lucy asked.

"Your favorite surfer girl Judy Leggett left me a lovely personal message. After letting me know she was at the airport about to board a plane for Puerto Vallarta, she announced that Bobby wasn't shot by any gardener named Max. Apparently that was the made-for-media version of reality. I don't know how she did it, she left that out of the message, but somehow she framed Max. And the reality of Bobby's death was quite a bit sleazier—or 'more intriguing,' in Judy's own words. She said Bobby was shot by the father of a fourteen-year-old girl, some Malibu nymphet whose Dad Bobby once did business with. He'd known this little chiquita all her life, apparently. Judy said Bobby was up at the saucer in bed with this girl and another one, also fourteen, when the father charged in, in an understandable rage, and shot him three times, in the face, the chest, and the groin, and then threw him off the cliff and drove off down the mountain with the two girls. Now that's ugly but it gets creepier still, because Judy said she was in a closet with a camera and got it all on tape and said that it was awesome footage. Then she said that she had been the one to call the dad to let him know where his little girl was that afternoon. And after that, she said, when she was sure Bobby was good and dead at the bottom of his very own cliff, she had called EMS to come save him."

Lucy was quiet for a few seconds. "Jesus, no wonder she and Maria were friends, or whatever you call people like that when they get together. They were peas in a pod."

"The Pod of Evil Incarnate," said Terry. "Who'd a thunk, heading off to Sayulita to crank out some high-priced verbiage for a made-for-TV surfing contest, that we would run into such despicable characters?" She sighed. "Well, Luce, the show's on in a couple days. You gonna watch?"

"Yes—but let's just say I'm not going to throw a party, know what I mean?"

"I do indeed. Let's compare notes afterwards, OK?"

"Deal."

Three days later, the *X Dames* reality-based TV movie, *Surf and Murder in Sayulita,* ran on the Outside Network on Saturday night at nine p.m., with a warning to parents about sexual content. Lucy insisted on watching it alone at home. The version that ran was surprisingly close to the one Mary had screened for them in LA, only they'd hired a better voice to do the narration. The high point of the whole thing had to be Marcia's aerial 360 high above the lip of a ten-foot wave face. Lucy found it totally embarrassing to see herself in a TV docu-movie, although several friends including Mickey, Robin, and, most importantly, Harold called right after it ended to tell her how great she looked. The sex scene Lucy had shot at Bobby's house was also included, although assorted crotches were digitally scrubbed. And finally, at last, the show ended with the question of guilt or innocence. Viewers were invited to call an 800 number and vote on whether anybody in the "cast" had conspired to commit murder, or had committed murder, and if so, who?

Lucy didn't bother to cast her vote. In the morning she got a call from Marcia, who told her she looked great before cutting to the real question: asking if Lucy's offer to put her up in New York was still good, as she had been accepted at the Pratt Art Institute, and also what did she think of "the verdict"? "Yes, of course you can stay here for a while," Lucy said. "And what was the verdict, by the way?"

The audience by an overwhelming majority had found Ruben Dario and Judy Leggett guilty of conspiracy to commit murder.

Lucy felt little or no satisfaction with this "verdict." After all, both of them, and possibly Maria as well, were down there, in Sayulita or somewhere farther south, tearing down pretty little houses to build big ugly apartment buildings, knocking people off if they got in the way, getting away with murder.

Marcia showed up. She and Lucy surfed Coney Island twice, waist-high waves but it was trippy riding the D train with surfboards. Marcia and Harold hit it off, although Lucy's sex life was temporarily limited to trysts in the love nook, as she'd named his little walk-up. She'd grown quite fond of it, once she got the loft back. And when Harold's neighbor Jack Verblonski died at the age of ninety-one in late September after sixty-seven years in the same apartment, Harold called in favors and bagged Marcia her own little East Village fourth floor walk-up, bath down the hall, tub in the kitchen, just like Harold's, for a rent-controlled, miraculously cheap four hundred a month.

They went out to celebrate with a dinner at one of the overpriced new French bistros on Ludlow Street. Afterwards Harold cited work to do, and Marcia cited unpacking to do, and so Lucy and Claud went home alone. She went up to the loft and turned on her laptop for a last look at her email before crashing. There was a message from Teresa in LA. She opened it.

> *Hey Luce: I've been working on this operation for a few weeks now, and forgive me for not including you from the get-go, but I wanted it to be a surprise. Check the link. I think you'll find it somewhat satisfying. Teresa.*

Lucy clicked on the link and found herself directed to a story that had been published that very morning on the *Los Angeles Times* Web site.

South of the Border,
Reality Catches Up to Reality TV

By Howard Stone

In a twist of fate sure to set tongues wagging from Hollywood to Mexico City, a reality-based TV movie that ran in late summer on cable has triggered a series of political and legal confrontations south of the border. The film, ostensibly a pilot for a reality series about women in extreme sports, called X Dames, *was made in Sayulita, a small town north of Puerto Vallarta on Mexico's Pacific Coast. Sayulita has become an increasingly popular vacation and second-home spot for Americans in recent years. Since it also has a fairly good surfing beach right in town, the* X Dames *producers selected it as their location for the first show, which was shot last spring with a surfing contest as the competitive event.*

However, during the show's surfing competition one of the contestants drowned under what some believed were suspicious circumstances. These circumstances—the death, by accident or murder, of American surfer Sandra Darwin—along with the contest, became part of the show, resulting in a fairly unusual bit of programming—a reality show with a real murder investigation worked into it. However, there was no legal action at the time, for reasons which were also included in the show. Instead, members of the audience were asked to decide who was guilty by calling an 800 number. Such audience votes are nothing new, but this one was slightly different in that there were, possibly, actual and serious crimes committed.

In light of that one of the show's writers, LA art critic Teresa MacDonald, was not satisfied with having only an audience find the guilty parties guilty. This was, after all, not only entertainment but reality. And so, MacDonald said she wanted "reality-based justice," meaning actual pursuit and arrest of those she believed to be the guilty parties—several of whom were involved in producing the show.

Thus, in an unprecedented and possibly illegal fashion, she "borrowed" a DVD of the show from director Mary Miles, made copies, and couriered them to several high-ranking government officials in Mexico City and Tepic, capital city of the province of Nayarit, where Sayulita is located. I watched the DVD recently, and it does include some thought-provoking questions about the death of Ms. Darwin, which has never been investigated by any legal authority. Ms. MacDonald, a recent recipient of a McClellan Fund grant, also wrote and sent a detailed explanation of the work she and her partner, New York writer Lucy Ripken, had done in investigating the case. Not in the least bit coincidentally, both writers played significant roles in the X Dames movie.

Several government officials in Mexico and Tepic viewed the film and read MacDonald's report. As a result, one Arturo Augustino Dario, *provincial head of the Federal Police for Nayarit, was removed from office. His replacement, Sergio Figueroa, wasted no time in seeking warrants for the arrest of several "characters" in the movie, namely Mexican-American real estate baron and sometime film producer Ruben Dario—not coincidentally the brother of the former Federales district chief Arturo Dario—and an American woman, Judith Leggett, a former surfing champion and one of the show's original producers (the other, Bobby Schamberg, recently died under suspicious circumstances at his Malibu home). Ms. Leggett currently calls Sayulita home. These two have been charged with conspiracy to commit murder, obstruction of justice, and real estate fraud, and are presently being held in the provincial jail in Tepic. Two others—a local doctor and another American woman surfer—face lesser charges. Another American who served as a producer on the film, Sophia Greenberg, is believed to be traveling in South America. Greenberg's role in the events that transpired in Sayulita remains unclear at this time, although Mr. Figueroa has described her as a "person of interest."*

The grace note came the next day, in the form of an email from Mariela Pastor, who wrote: *I do not know how you do this, Lucy, but thank you for stopping them. They were going to begin to tear down Sandra's house in two days' time, but the police have taken Ruben Dario and Judy Leggett away and Señor Townsend has decided he will return to the United States. Muchas Gracias, Mariela. ps If ever you wish to come here you can stay with us, please. Mariela.*

The biggest problem in Lucy's world remained at large, in South America, with a remodeled face and revenge in her heart. Otherwise, all was well for the moment.